"I woke up naked..."

Calla's face turned pink. "I thought you'd be more comfortable out of your clothes."

Devin did more for a black T-shirt and jeans than anybody she knew, but the view beneath the cotton was exponentially better. Not that she'd looked. For long.

And he was still caressing her hand. She inched toward him. Yes, he was worried—even if he didn't want to admit he was. It would be wrong, very wrong, to take advantage of him in his current state.

And yet her libido was also needy and it was whispering seductively about the possibility of this being her one and only opportunity to be with him.

Before her conscience could talk sense to her, or he could think quickly enough to shove her away, she wrapped her arms around his neck and pressed her lips to his.

Desperate as the move was, it was worth the reward.

He crushed her against him, bracing his hand at the back of her head to hold her in place as he drove his tongue past her lips. Her senses ignited, and he fanned the flames, consuming her like a man starved for air.

Finally, was all she could think.

Blaze

Dear Reader,

So our Robin Hood gang is back, and this time the tables are turned. After two adventures, two solved cases and two loving relationships, a new threat has invaded to exact its own brand of justice—on Devin, our hero.

I had always planned Calla and Devin's romance this way. I wanted the friends—Calla, Shelby and Victoria—to experience success by taking the initiative at righting wrongs, by making a positive difference in their lives and the lives of others. But the concept of what's right and wrong with society, and who gets to decide, isn't as simple as it often seems.

Challenging one's moral code—in real life or fiction—brings out the best and worst in all of us. And that's exactly what Calla and Devin are faced with before they, too, can find their happily-ever-after.

Happy reading!

Wendy

Wendy Etherington

UNDONE BY MOONLIGHT

HARLEQUIN®

entertain, enrich, inspire™

Recycling programs
for this product may
not exist in your area.

ISBN-13: 978-0-373-79713-4

UNDONE BY MOONLIGHT

This edition published by arrangement with Harlequin Books S.A.

For questions and comments about the quality of this book please contact us at CustomerService@Harlequin.com.

www.Harlequin.com

Printed in U.S.A.

ABOUT THE AUTHOR

Wendy Etherington was born and raised in the deep South—and she has the fried-chicken recipes and NASCAR ticket stubs to prove it. An author of nearly thirty books, she writes full-time from her home in South Carolina, where she lives with her husband, two daughters and an energetic shih tzu named Cody. She can be reached via her website, www.wendyetherington.com. Or follow her on Twitter @wendyeth.

Books by Wendy Etherington

HARLEQUIN BLAZE
263—JUST ONE TASTE...
310—A BREATH AWAY
385—WHAT HAPPENED IN VEGAS...
446—AFTER DARK
524—TEMPT ME AGAIN
562—HER PRIVATE TREASURE
587—IRRESISTIBLE FORTUNE
684—SIZZLE IN THE CITY*
697—BREATHLESS AT THE BEACH*

HARLEQUIN NASCAR
HOT PURSUIT
FULL THROTTLE
NO HOLDING BACK (with Liz Allison)
RISKING HER HEART (with Liz Allison)

*Flirting with Justice

To law enforcement everywhere.
Your sacrifice and dedication are appreciated.

"The law condemns and punishes only actions within certain definite and narrow limits; it thereby justifies, in a way, all similar actions that lie outside those limits."

—Leo Tolstoy, *What I Believe*

1

The New York Tattletale
October 12th

Lions and Tigers and Scandal Among the NYPD
by Peeps Galloway, Gossipmonger
(And proud of it!)

Oh, Dear Reader, one of our own has fallen.

And fallen hard.

Detective Devin Antonio (highlighted in *this* column last spring and summer!) has been mysteriously suspended.

Apparently (Oh, my, don't you just *love* that word?) he found himself at the scene of a robbery last night. The suspect was apparently (there it is again) escaping as the detective arrived, so he apparently (oh, joy!) felt the need to not only slap on the handcuffs, but also use his size and prowess to subdue and control the situation.

I'm shocked and downtrodden. I'm horrified and sympathetic. I'm literally unable to get out of bed.

Kidding!

Though, NYPD, I'm, of course, on your side. I stand for truth and justice above all.

Apparently, there are some secrets in the great detective's past he failed to share with those most important in his life. Will this derail his flirtations with a certain travel writer he's been seen around town with? Will this get him (gasp) fired?

As documented in *this* column, he's helped solve some high-profile crimes over the last several months, including the Jenkins Scandal and the Rutherford Theft. But those triumphs are unlikely to sway the D.A., who's *apparently* tired of explaining to the attorney general about why corruption is so prevalent on our beloved island of Manhattan.

Maybe a hotel heiress or two will do something more scandalous next week…though I'm not counting on it. (Kidding again! I *so* am!)

Stay tuned for more *apparently* bad behavior and (please, oh, please) more hot cops,
—*Peeps*

I dream of you day and night.

"YEAH, YEAH," CALLA Tucker muttered at the text message she'd received nearly a month ago and had yet to erase.

She couldn't imagine brooding detective Devin Antonio had actually meant the words. And if, by some miracle, he had, he probably hadn't meant them for her.

Of course her sarcastic response, Are you feeling okay? hadn't helped matters. He hadn't responded to that question at all, and when she'd tried to talk to him about the message, he'd acted as if he hadn't known what she was talking about.

Yet she'd left her best friend's wedding reception early because he hadn't shown up as he'd promised and now she was scooting around Manhattan in a cab, racking up a fare that she was going to need a loan to pay for, simply because she was worried about him.

"You want me to wait again?" the cabbie asked as he pulled up to the police station.

She glanced at the amount, winced, then handed the driver a wad of cash. "No, thanks. I think this is my last stop."

She'd already called Devin's cell phone and sent half a dozen text messages, checked his apartment and phoned Paddy's bar across the street from the precinct house—his usual haunt—all with no results. If he wasn't at work, she was out of ideas.

Wearing a full-length, navy blue taffeta bridesmaid's dress and a sprinkling of white flowers in her hair, she got a number of stares and two whistles before she yanked open the door and strode inside.

"I need to see Detective Antonio, please," she said to the bored-looking clerk, snapping gum as she lorded over the small, dingy waiting room from behind a high, faded-wood counter.

The clerk tapped on her computer, then announced, "Antonio's off duty."

He certainly promised to take the day off, Calla thought peevishly. And if a luxurious and wildly romantic wedding didn't get him to finally make a move on her, she wasn't sure anything would do the trick.

And yet, here she was, making an idiot of herself chasing after him.

"What about Lieutenant Meyer?" she asked the clerk.

This got a reaction. Staring down at Calla, the clerk raised her eyebrows—which were dyed purple. "You got an appointment?"

"No, but he's a good friend." She reached into her bag and pulled out the piece of cake she'd put in a plastic baggie to bring to Devin. "A mutual friend of ours got married tonight, so I brought him some cake."

Along with her proof of friendship, she gave the clerk a broad smile.

In return, she received a narrow-eyed glare.

Having lived in New York for six years, Calla knew she should be used to this kind of suspicious response by now. But she was from Texas, for heaven's sake. Beauty queen smiles and big blond hair were both a birthright and an entrée into any event, anytime. She had no idea how to deal with Purple Eyebrow People.

"What color is that?" the clerk asked suddenly.

Calla shifted her gaze to the cake. "My friend Shelby insisted on making her own wedding cake and really wanted the roses to be aqua, but I think they came out icy-green. Still it's—"

"On your head," the clerk clarified.

"Oh. It's a mix of golden-blond with champagne highlights. I had a great girl who did it back in Texas, but it was a challenge to find somebody here who didn't charge three hundred dollars." She leaned closer, so she wouldn't be overheard. A woman's stylist was a private matter, after all. "Eventually, I found this great color specialist named Kirk. He's at Tangles on Bleecker in the West Village. Tell him Calla sent you, and he'll give you a ten-percent discount."

"Cool."

An instant later, the door to Calla's right buzzed as

the clerk released the lock leading to the station's inner sanctum.

Connections. This town was all about connections.

With a bit more confidence—something she sorely needed to counteract the prissy flowers in her hair—she walked down the hall toward the squad room where Devin's desk was located. The couple of times she'd been there, she'd noticed his lieutenant's office in the corner. Devin had always spoken pretty highly of his boss, which meant he'd grunted and shrugged when she'd asked what it was like to work for Meyer.

Knocking tentatively on the closed door, she jolted when a deep, authoritative voice called out, "Come in!"

The office was fairly small, containing a wooden desk, a guest chair and a bookcase packed haphazardly with magazines and stacks of papers. A man of about fifty with dark brown hair graying at the temples sat behind the desk. He started to give her an impatient stare, but his expression turned into a charming smile as his gaze raked her body. He rose. "Can I help you?"

At least *somebody* was happy to see her. "I'm looking for Detective Antonio."

The smile disappeared. "He's not here."

"So they told me out front. I was hoping you'd know where he was. He promised he'd come to my friend's wedding, but he didn't show up. He's not at home, and he won't answer his phone. I'm worried."

"Antonio can take care of himself."

"I'm sure he can. Mind if I sit?" She dropped into the guest chair before he could refuse. "How about some cake?" she asked, holding out the piece she'd shown the reception clerk.

With a sigh, he sat behind his desk and took the cake. "You're his girlfriend?" he asked.

Well, I've been trying... "No, just a friend."

Meyer said nothing for several moments. "You have a boyfriend?"

"No."

"I always thought Antonio was a sharp guy." He shrugged. "Truth is, he's been suspended."

Calla felt the blood drain from her face. "Since when?"

"A couple hours ago."

Explaining why he'd bailed on the wedding. But he could have called her. Maybe she and her *gang*—as he liked to call her and her friends Shelby and Victoria—could help. "For what?"

"I'm sorry, I can't say. It's an internal matter."

"How much trouble is he in?"

"A lot."

"He could lose his job?"

"Definitely."

Though Devin was closemouthed about his feelings, his life, his past, well, pretty much everything, she knew he valued being a cop above everything else. "But he's a great cop."

"I think so."

"Then why—" She stopped as the lieutenant shook his head. He wouldn't budge. "Any idea where I can find him?"

"Try Paddy's."

"Already did."

"O'Leary's Pub, then. Two blocks east."

"Thanks," she said, rising.

He flashed a bright smile. "Anytime."

Even though she wore four-inch heels, Calla walked to the pub.

Hadn't she strutted across dozens of pageant stages?

Hadn't she paid her way through college with said pageant scholarship winnings and graduated at the top of her journalism class? Hadn't she made a life for herself in the media capital of the world?

So why was her stomach clenched at the thought of seeing Devin? At the confrontation to come?

Gee, Calla, can't imagine why you'd be nervous.

Maybe because she knew he'd been suspended before. A fact he'd told her, almost offhand, though he'd refused to give details.

Being naturally as well as professionally nosy, she'd researched his revelation six months ago. She'd discovered little about the cause for his punishment. *Personal reasons relating to an open case* was the official line, and Devin, being such an effusive guy—ha, ha— had, naturally, not filled in the blanks. With little to go on, and out of character for her, she'd been intimidated to probe him further about his clearly painful past.

Apparently that day had now come.

She was looking forward to challenging that Irish-and-Italian temper. *Ha ha.*

She nearly walked by O'Leary's before noticing the ancient-looking oak door. *B' fhearr liom uisce beatha* was burned into a plank of wood above the arched entrance. Something Gaelic, she'd imagine.

And possibly threatening, she added as she opened the door and saw the tiny, barely lit interior of the place and its patrons. If possible, it was a step down, as well as infinitely darker, than Devin's usual hangout.

Why couldn't the man have a beer at Applebee's once in a while?

Movement in the bar ground to a halt.

So distracted with worrying over Devin being suspended—again—she'd forgotten about her bridesmaid outfit. She really should have taken the time to change before racing off on this crazy quest.

Head held high, she moved across the room, wishing for a flashlight instead of the fireplace along the back wall as she searched in vain for Devin. The wooden floor beneath her feet was rough and uneven in places, and her new shoes had little traction. If she tripped amid all these suspicious stares and snarls of disapproval, the detective wouldn't have to worry about his job, as his autopsy photos would be Exhibit A at her murder trial.

"Antonio?" she asked the bartender, pleased her voice didn't tremble.

Heavyset with razor sharp eyes, he said nothing and pointed to the back corner of the room.

Where else?

Bracing herself, she carefully picked her way around the tables. As she got closer, she saw the gleam of his black hair reflected by the old-fashioned lantern on the wall next to him. He was hunched over a tumbler of what was certainly whiskey, his long fingers rhythmically stroking the sides of the glass.

Her heart contracted. Desire invaded her as she focused on his hands, the concentrated stare, the care with which he touched, as she imagined he'd caress her skin.

When she stopped beside his table, he looked up. His green eyes, so in contrast to his bronzed skin, pierced her, and she swore he could see through her into every fantasy she'd ever had about him.

And there were a number to choose from.

She'd lost her mind. She wanted him without reason. He was wounded, and she was going to save him. Like the stray cats, dogs and even birds she'd taken in as a child, she'd tend and encourage until he could move freely in his own world.

He'd given her little-to-zero motivation except for a few hot looks and riding to the rescue when she and her friends had asked him for help.

But she also couldn't forget the text. For her? Or for someone else? Regardless, the emotion behind the message and the possibility of them together dangled before her like a carrot she couldn't look away from, couldn't deny she craved.

Oh, yeah, she'd lost her mind.

She shivered with delight as he wrapped his fingers around her wrist and tugged her into the chair beside him. Finally, finally, he was going to give in to the desire crackling the air whenever they were together. She had no idea why he'd held back, but that didn't matter anymore. They could—

"Are you an angel?" he asked, his voice slurred just before he pressed his lips to the racing pulse beneath her jaw.

Terrific. He was completely trashed.

Her fantasy went up in a puff of smoke.

Though the movement cost her a great deal, she jerked her head away. "It's Calla," she said firmly. Swallowing her pride when his face remained dazed, she added, "Calla Tucker."

"Calla," he murmured and she swore she got a buzz from his breath as he leaned toward her. "I missed you."

"Do you dream of me?" she couldn't help asking.

"Always."

His mouth moved across her cheek toward her lips, and she closed her eyes as need washed over her. With an exquisite gentleness she'd never imagined him capable of, he cupped her jaw in his palm and laid his lips over hers.

He slid his tongue into her mouth, stroking, enticing...promising. She gave in return. For a single moment in time, she enjoyed his single-focused attention and passion. Still, she wanted more.

But not like this.

She pulled away when he would have let the kiss go on. She scooted her chair back to extend the distance.

His striking eyes were muddled. He was troubled and confused. She wouldn't let him stay there.

"I had cake," she blurted, "but I had to trade it to find you."

A light shone from within. "Cake?"

"From Shelby and Trevor's wedding. Remember? You were supposed to be there."

"Yeah, she's nice, and she can cook. I was at the hospital. Sorry."

She tensed. "Hospital?"

"Last night anyway." He cocked his head, looking lost. "Or maybe this morning."

"What happened?" Her gaze flew over him, searching for wounds. "How were you hurt?"

He turned, revealing a white bandage on the back of his head. "Knocked out."

"When?"

"Last night." Again, he angled his head as if remembering required a great deal of thought. "Or maybe this morning."

She was fairly certain that a man who'd sustained a head wound in the past twenty-four hours hadn't been prescribed alcohol. Snatching his half-full tumbler before he could take another sip, she grabbed his hand. "You should be home in bed, not here."

"Bed?" He grinned. "If you say so…"

Her carnal and practical sides were officially at war. She should reject him; she should comfort him. She wanted him; she hated what he was doing to himself.

She'd seen him have a beer or a glass of whiskey, but she'd never imagined him so out of control, leaving himself so vulnerable. So susceptible to despair.

"Bed to sleep," she said to him. "You have to rest."

"I'll rest when I'm dead."

"Yes, well, I imagine that glorious moment isn't too far away." She tugged him to a shaky stand, then guided him to the bar. "We need a cab," she said to the bartender.

Clearly, he didn't like a woman taking control in his manly establishment as he cast a glance at Devin, then back at her. "He seems fine to me."

"I'll have—" Devin's head drooped and only Calla holding him up kept him from collapsing to the floor.

"Sure." Calla grunted under the weight propping up Devin. "He's fine. On the other hand, I know a really good lawyer…."

The bartender held her gaze, unblinking, and she had long enough to consider how she'd escape the bar with a half-conscious Devin without help. Considering the barkeep's hard, dark brown stare, she quickly amended her worry to *without permission.*

"Yeah, yeah," he grumbled, picking up the phone receiver behind the bar. After a brief conversation, he turned to her. "Cab'll be here in a minute."

"Great. Thanks. But it'll take me at least ten to drag him to the door." She gave him her best beauty queen smile. "Any chance you could give me a hand?"

With an ill-tempered sigh, he rounded the bar and

shouldered half of Devin's weight. Together, they partly walked, partly dragged him to the door.

Bleary-eyed, Devin's head swayed from Calla to the bartender. "Babe, you're really hot, but I'm not doin' a three-way with another dude."

Oh, good grief.

"I'll try to contain my disappointment," she said dryly.

Once their odd trio stumbled their way through the open door and onto the sidewalk, a cab was waiting at the curb. With the bartender's help, Calla managed to tuck Devin into the taxi. From her tasseled bag—a dead match to her dress—she dug out twenty bucks and handed her helper the money.

"His bill was fifty," he growled.

"Of course it was." Reaching back in her bag, she came up with two more twenties, which she handed him before he ambled back inside the bar.

She dearly hoped the cabbie took credit cards. Plus, she was picking Devin's pocket the moment she got him horizontal. And that was all she was doing. Well, after groping his firm-looking butt.

Damn. She was back in fantasyland.

Though, with her flowers, cake and taffeta, she looked more suited to a game of Candyland, while Devin looked as if he was in the midst of escaping Call of Duty, the Hellfire and Brimstone version.

"I live on West 22nd Street," Devin mumbled when she climbed inside the car. He dropped his head into her lap. "Near the museum."

"I know." Unable to resist running her fingers through Devin's silky hair, she gave the cabbie the exact address. "How do you afford to live there on a detective's salary, by the way?"

"My landlord gives a break to cops." His hand slid down her dress. "How long is this thing?" Basically answering his own question, she felt him reach the hem and start gliding his fingers up, under the the taffeta this time.

While trying not to focus on the fact that several dreams she'd spent months dwelling on were currently coming true, she realized a big flaw in her plan.

How was she going to get him horizontal to grope him? And, worse, how was she going to get him from the cab to the elevator? Though in a nice neighborhood, Devin's apartment didn't lean toward a doorman. She was out of cash to bribe the cabbie with.

She could call her friends, but two of them were on their way to their honeymoon in Switzerland and the other two—if she knew Victoria and her boyfriend, Jared, well enough—were already celebrating on their own by now.

She asked the cabbie to head to her apartment instead of Devin's. At least there she was pretty sure she could find a neighbor to help.

"Your place?" Devin asked. "How big is the bed?"

"Big enough."

The tips of Devin's fingers brushed her panties. "Whoa, Detective," she said, clamping her thighs together. "We barely know each other. Let's commit a few misdemeanors before we move on to felonies."

"Calla," he breathed. "I know you."

Closing her eyes, she swallowed. What had she done to deserve this torture? How long had she dreamed of him touching her, wanting her?

"Already did felony assault," Devin mumbled.

"You— What?"

He ran his hand across her upper thigh. "Glad you

dumped that other guy. We can have a good time all on our own."

And yet she had the feeling he'd pass out long before her "good time" was fully realized. "Felony assault?"

"Some guy. Didn't hit him. He hit me." His fingers dug briefly into her skin. "He can't come to bed with us, either."

She patted his back. "Fine. You, me, bed. Felony assault?"

"Shoulda been. No score, though."

"What score?"

"Yankees lost. Lost twenty bucks on those bums."

"Devin, please." She grabbed his hand as it again inched toward the juncture of her thighs. "Focus. Who hit you?"

"Somebody hit me?" He lifted his head, which he laid against her breast. "Had to be me, I guess. The Yankees sure aren't gettin' enough. They'd need a damn GPS to find the ball. How 'bout a little TLC?"

As his lips moved against her neck, she fought back the tide of desire.

This was getting her nowhere. Drunk and concussed people didn't have coherent conversations. She needed to get him home and into bed. She should probably call the hospital and find out what the doctor had actually told him to do to care for his injury, since she couldn't imagine bellying up to the bar was listed on the discharge papers.

Still, she had one question left that she was positive he could answer. "The sign above the door at the pub, what does it mean?"

"I would prefer whiskey."

Of course he did.

2

DEVIN ROLLED OVER, and his head throbbed in retaliation.

"I'm supposed to be dead," he groaned.

His mouth felt as though somebody had filled it full of cotton. His body was stiff; his energy level was depleted by the rolling. And had he mentioned the head-throbbing?

Then he smelled her.

Calla. So full of hope and brightness.

Her warm vanilla scent surrounded him, comforting even though he didn't deserve solace or sympathy. Maybe he had something to live for, after all.

Flashes of the night before, however, returned in a wave of panic and humiliation. Snippets of conversation about cake, three-ways and hits. Whether those were mob hits or his continual focus on the Yankees' lousy batting average, he wasn't sure. Him kissing her, shoving his hand beneath her skirt.

Please, oh, please, tell me I didn't actually do that.

Course the Almighty wasn't listening as a wave of nausea turned his stomach. Not that he deserved mercy regardless.

He chanced opening his eyes, surprised when no further pain assaulted him. The room was dark, with only a strip of light shining under the door and a star-shaped night-light plugged into the wall to his right.

Hold everything.

This wasn't his apartment, and he certainly wasn't in his bed. Squinting, he could make out the white-and-pink rose-laden comforter covering him. Beneath the sheet—also pink—he was naked.

Oh, man. Oh, no. Please. No.

Guilt shot through every cell in his body. Surely he hadn't had sex with her. He wouldn't have taken advantage of her that way. Not even he could have done that.

Fear drove him from the bed. Each movement caused his stomach to roll and his head to pound, but he gritted his teeth and kept going. He was in the midst of figuring out what he could wear when he saw his clothes neatly folded on the dresser.

He wasn't sure what that level of care said, but knew he shouldn't think about the implications too long.

And yet, the dread that he'd given into his baser needs with Calla when he'd promised himself not to go near her was nearly overwhelmed by the anxiety that she was, even now, planning their wedding. Both scenarios gave him the motivation to stumble into the bathroom, splash water on his face and hair, rinse with the mouthwash he found beneath the sink, get dressed then crack the bedroom door.

Immediately, he smelled bacon.

Surprisingly, his stomach whimpered with need. If he could get his hands on that bacon, a gallon of coffee and four or ten aspirin, he might make it through the day.

With a confidence he didn't feel, he strode through

the living room to the bar-high counter bordering the kitchen.

Wearing a robe the color of cotton candy, she stood in front of the stove. Her tanned and toned legs peaked from beneath the robe's hem. Her long blond hair was piled on top of her head in a messy mass that turned him on in a big way.

But then wasn't everything associated with her arousing?

"Bacon?" he managed to croak.

She smiled at him over her shoulder. "I thought I heard water running. Pretty fast shower."

"I didn't take a shower."

The smile turned to a scowl. "Why not? I put out fresh soap and shampoo. Not my girly stuff, either."

"I'm probably in your way."

"You're not. Don't you want bacon?" When he nodded, she added, "Breakfast will take a few more minutes. Plenty of time for a shower."

"Don't you have work to do?"

"It's Sunday. Wanna take a shower or tell me about last night?"

He headed back to the bedroom. In the shower, he acknowledged the hot, powerful spray from overhead cleared much of his confusion.

One, sex between him and Calla was still imaginary. A realization that was both good and bad.

Two, his head didn't hurt just because he'd overindulged in whiskey. He'd been whacked on the back of the head. Reaching behind him, he found a bandage and smooth skin around the edges. Hell. Somebody'd shaved a section of his head. He wasn't vain about stuff like that but still...a bald spot?

Not only did he not have game, his game was on strike.

For the shaving and bandage, he recalled a hospital nurse. For the assault he drew a blank.

He shook his head, which did nothing but increase the incessant pounding.

Bracing his forehead against the tiled shower stall, he fought to push through the clouds clogging his memory, but the deluge of water only made him wonder if he was supposed to get his bandage wet, and, if he did, would he die of an antibiotic-resistant bacterial infection or simply start leaking brain fluid that would swirl down the drain?

And, if so, would that please happen now?

Until one of those glorious moments occurred, he might as well make the woman who promised to feed him happy. He reached for the mini hotel shampoo she'd obviously set out for him, but was distracted by the large bottles belonging to her. Leaning close, he inhaled vanilla and sugar and his head immediately stopped pounding.

Contentment washed over him, even as hunger to be near her ran rampant. She'd tempted him for months, even though he knew they couldn't be together. She was too bright and pure, and he wasn't about to drag her into his crappy life and past.

He resisted the urge to cover himself in her scent and washed quickly with the hotel-size green tea products. Once he'd dressed and headed toward the kitchen a second time, he acknowleged she'd been right. The shower had steadied him.

Course a lot of his memory was muddled, and that was going to be a problem. From past experience, he knew she was relentless when she was after something.

He sure didn't think she'd let him get away with a free breakfast and hot shower.

As he walked from the bedroom toward the kitchen, she was dishing scrambled eggs onto a plate already groaning with bacon. His stomach grumbled in response.

"How do you take your coffee?" she asked in a cheerful, if low volume, voice.

His pounding head appreciated the care. Why was she so good to him when he didn't deserve to be in the same room with her? "Black, thanks."

He sat on one of the two stools pushed up against the bar bracketing the kitchen on two sides. She handed him a heavy-looking mug, though he imagined her cupboards were full of dainty teacups. A quick scan of the counter proved his guess—a cream scallop-edged cup with a bouquet of pink roses decorating the side sat beside the stove.

As he took the first sip of coffee, their gazes locked. Weak as he was, he quickly looked away. He didn't need to complicate his already tangled life with his confusing feelings for her.

The silence lingered until she set a filled plate on the bar before him. Maybe he could slink away, after all.

But he'd barely taken his first bite when she slid onto the stool next to him and asked, "So, wanna tell me about last night?"

"No."

"Sure?"

"Very."

She pushed a small glass filled with orange juice toward him. "This will help."

Shrugging, he drank the juice in a quick swallow.

As soon as he set the empty glass on the bar, she

pushed another one in his line of vision. This one held tomato juice, complete with celery stalk artistically leaning against the side.

He curled his lip. "I don't like—"

"Drink it."

As he often found in her presence, he did as she ordered, though he would swear he hadn't made a conscious decision to do so.

Surprisingly, the juice wasn't bland, watery tomatoes. The drink had a spicy kick, as if she'd made a Bloody Mary without the shot of vodka. Though he had a feeling, based on the determined look on her face, that he could use the added buzz.

"The vitamins in oranges, tomatoes and celery are good for you," she said.

He also had the feeling she'd told him that before. Not surprising. This wasn't his first ride around the block with hangovers. "Goody. You know how I like to take care of myself."

"Eat the celery." When he started to argue, she added, "Think of the celery as a carrot for the bacon reward."

He chomped the stalk in two bites, then grabbed two slices of bacon from the plate before she could come up with some other healthy barrier to his fat-laden breakfast.

His obedience bought him silence, as she said nothing while he inhaled the food.

"You're not eating?" he asked when he paused long enough to notice she wasn't.

"I had a spinach omelet earlier."

In his opinion, the only place for something green in eggs was in children's stories that rhyme. But also knowing she'd go back to the subject of last night, he commented, "You've got a nice place."

"Thanks. Because of all my pageant winnings, I went to college on a full scholarship, so my parents gave me the money they'd been saving for school."

"Pageant? Like bikini contest?" He could certainly imagine her figure earning piles of cash.

"No, like Miss America. You know, evening gowns, crowns and sashes, questions about world peace."

She was a beauty queen; he was a master marksman. If ever two people were less compatible, he couldn't imagine who, when or where. "You have a lot of roses in here."

"When your name is a flower, you have to go with it."

"So why not lilies?"

"Too obvious. You're not going to divert my attention from asking about last night, by the way."

"I figured it was worth a shot."

"How about if we start with an easy question? Who hit you over the head?"

He shook his head. "No idea."

"Okay, not a good start."

"Everything's pretty fuzzy."

"I'll bet. How 'bout we start from the beginning? What's the last thing you remember clearly?"

He struggled to think back. "I picked up my suit from the dry cleaners." His only suit, come to think of it.

"You were coming to the wedding," Calla said, gazing at him with wonder.

"I was invited."

"So you were. After dry cleaning?"

"Hung around my apartment awhile, fixed my neighbor's ceiling fan, then went to the bar down the street to watch football."

When he stopped, she asked, "Did you get into an argument with somebody at the bar?"

"No, I—" *What?* He recalled watching the Syracuse-Rutgers game of all things, but had no idea what happened afterward.

"Try to picture yourself."

When he did, he was rewarded with a sharp jab of pain to the back of his skull. Wincing, he shook his head.

She slid off her stool. "Why don't you take one of your pain pills? You've eaten now, so you can—"

"What pain pills?"

"The ones the E.R. doctor prescribed, but you didn't pick up, instead choosing to drown yourself in whiskey." She pursed her lips in censure. "Which was not prescribed, by the way."

He grabbed her wrist as she started off. "No, thanks. They'll make my thoughts even more jumbled." He realized he was touching her when heat shot up his arm. He let go immediately and picked up his coffee mug. "Thanks for getting them, though. I'll pay you back."

She returned to her seat, and he got a mouth-watering glimpse of her upper thigh. "You're racking up quite a tab."

Tab. He pausing before drinking the coffee. "I paid my tab at the bar and left. I headed down the street… toward my apartment, but I saw…something."

"Somebody you knew?"

Automatically, he shook his head. He didn't think he'd talked to anybody. Since he wasn't much on conversation, he was fairly certain he'd remember having one. Hell, he could have tripped over a damn dog and banged his head on the sidewalk for all he knew.

But even a bungling move like that wouldn't have sent him to drown his sorrows at O'Leary's.

"Somebody hit you," she said, breaking into his thoughts.

Startled, he stared at her. "How do you—"

"You told me last night. You weren't sure at first whether you'd gotten hit or the Yankees lost 'cause they couldn't, but since a picture of the Yankees manager kicking home plate is on the front page of the sports section, and you've got a bandage and a headache, I'm pretty sure you were the one involved in hitting."

Sometimes, for no reason at all, he found himself tempted to smile at her. "You'd make quite a detective."

"No, thanks, the job perils are a little steep for me. Who'd hit a cop?"

He shrugged. He had some basic assault cases pending on his desk, but nothing that would warrant clobbering a cop. And it'd been years since he'd made the mistake of sleeping with a married woman.

Job. She'd jarred his memory again. He'd been doing his job after the bar. He had a vague picture of a short, dark-haired guy wearing a ball cap and overcoat running down an alley. He told as much to Calla.

"Why was he running?" she asked.

"He was a thief?" he asked rather than said, though the reason sounded right.

"How did you know he was a thief?"

"He was running away." But he hadn't worn his uniform since the swearing-in ceremony two years ago when he'd made detective. How had the guy made him for a cop? Or had he? "He had a bag, a red lady's handbag," he said finally as a flash of the scene came back to him. "I was pissed cause I had to chase him. I knew I'd be late for the wedding if I had to arrest him."

He'd known Calla would be furious. Plus, he'd wanted to see her in her bridesmaid's dress.

"Did you catch him?"

"No. Everything goes black then."

"That's when you got hit."

"I guess."

"We can be fairly certain. The ambulance picked up you and another man from an alley." When he looked questioningly at her, she added, "After you passed out last night, I made a few phone calls."

He recalled a ride in an ambulance, EMTs snapping orders, the scream of sirens, flashing lights. His memory also provided a vision of his purse snatcher's battered face. Why was that so vivid and yet he only got a fuzzy image of Calla in her bridesmaid's dress?

Life isn't fair, Antonio. You ought to know that by now.

"I called the ambulance," he said slowly, sliding off his stool to pace the living room floor. The pieces were falling into place, and the picture they formed wasn't pretty. "When I woke up, my suspect was unconscious next to me and beat all to hell. We were alone."

Calla angled her head. "So somebody hit you, then ran him down, attacked him, dragged him next to you and left you both there bleeding?"

The fact that she hadn't immediately wondered if *he'd* beaten the suspect was a loyalty he had no idea how he could have earned. Along with anger and worry, something sweet and pure shot through him.

Something he had no business enjoying.

"Pretty implausible, right?" he commented.

"It actually seems like the only explanation. Conversely, it also explains—" She paused, her gaze jumping to his.

"Why I've been suspended?"

She bit her lip. "Remembered that, have you?"

"The whole rosy scene is fairly clear now. How do you know? Another one of your phone calls?"

"I went to see Lieutenant Meyer when you didn't show up at the wedding. That's how I found you at the bar." She crossed her arms over her chest, looking like an outraged fairy. "He honestly thinks you beat up a suspect then knocked yourself out?"

"I'm not sure what he thinks, but since that's the story my purse snatcher told the cops, I've been suspended pending investigation of his assault."

Calla's jaw dropped. "The thief told them you beat him up?"

"Yep."

"But you were knocked out, too. Who's investigating *your* assault?"

He sneered. "I imagine that's pretty low on the list of priority cases."

3

CALLA SLAMMED THE skillet in the sink and began to scrub, though she knew it was ridiculous to dream that Devin's mess could be so easily cleaned up. "This is outrageous. Meyer's taking the word of some two-bit, scummy purse snatcher over one of his own detectives?"

"Probably not," Devin said, still pacing, even though he had to be dizzy by now. "But the incident has to be investigated. You gotta admit the whole thing is strange. The suspect—who Meyer referred to as a witness, by the way—says I started chasing him for no reason, then whaled on him once I caught him in the alley. And nobody found a purse on him. He had his own wallet in his back pocket, and that was it."

"Obviously whoever hit both of you took it."

"That much has occurred to me in the last few minutes. But unless this mysterious attacker shows up and confesses, the lieutenant has an investigation to run. I'm a suspect and out of the department until he does."

"Heaven forbid he should stand by you."

"He has to stay impartial. Dirty cops are serious business. I'm sure Internal Affairs will be knocking on my door very soon."

Awaiting him there were Calla, Shelby and Howard Bleaker, munchkin attorney-at-law.

Devin's supposedly passionless heart leaped with joy at seeing his gorgeous blond lover, but his eyes couldn't help but take in all of Howard. He was a tiny guy with brown, bowl-cut hair and dark-rimmed glasses that dominated his face. He looked more like someone who should be in math class at MIT than arguing points of law in front of a jury.

"Devin. Thank heaven you're—" Calla charged toward him, grinding to a halt as she no doubt noticed the cuffs. Panic and anger leaped into her eyes. "What's going on?"

"Can I have a minute?" Devin asked Reid.

"You have to be processed before—"

"Of course you can," Calla interrupted, shooting Reid a violent glare. "I brought your lawyer."

Clearing his throat, Howard stepped forward to address Reid. "My client is a duly designated officer of the law. Handcuffs are hardly necessary."

"They are when you're arrested," Reid returned. "As you should know, Counselor."

"I'll need copies of all the charges and statements immediately," Howard said, not missing a beat.

Reid inclined his head. "You'll have them."

"I also need to consult with my client."

"After he's processed."

Howard shook his head, and Devin had to give the little guy points for standing firm. "Now."

Reid sighed. "Fine." He unlocked the cuffs, then opened the interrogation room door. "Five minutes."

The whole exchange had happened so fast Devin was alone with Calla and the lawyer he didn't even recall hiring before remembering he'd specifically told Calla not to call Howard.

However, he'd also told her he wasn't under arrest.

Calla threw her arms around him. "How did this happen? What's Reid thinking? What are they saying you did? They can't really think you beat up Forrester. This isn't right!"

Devin absorbed her warmth and inhaled the scent of her vanilla-ladened shampoo. Had it only been a few hours ago he'd woken in her bed? Since they'd shared breakfast, sighs and secrets?

Howard captured her hand and pulled her away from Devin. "It's okay, Calla. We'll figure this out. Let the man breathe."

Devin tugged her back into his arms. "I like her where she is."

For good measure, he tossed a hard look at his lawyer. They might as well be clear from the start—Devin might not deserve Calla, but she belonged to him, and Two-Date Howard wasn't getting in the middle.

Calla laid her palm against his cheek. "How possessive of you."

"I listen. Mostly, anyway," he added when recalling she'd been right about needing legal advice sooner than later. "You're sure about Howard?"

"Juries like him. They find him nonthreatening."

"As long as you don't find him hot."

As an answer, she placed a quick kiss on his lips, then stepped back. "I realize you two know each other, but we should make it official. Howard, this is Detective Devin Antonio. Devin, Howard Bleaker, your attorney."

Shaking Howard's hand, Devin overlooked the detail of him never actually having hired hiring a lawyer. Mostly because, much as he hated to admit it, he needed help. But probably because he couldn't say no to her. What mortal man could?

"What are they charging you with?" Howard asked, laying his briefcase on the desk.

"Assault." Devin rubbed the back of his head. A headache was coming on. As the doctor warned, they happened with little urging these days, and his current scrape was a guaranteed trigger. "It's a long story."

"We'll give you the details at my place later," Calla said. "We're assembling the team now. Can you get Devin bailed today?"

Howard blinked. Was he confused by the question, or momentarily dazzled by Calla's golden splendor? "Shouldn't be a problem," he said finally, taking a notepad from his briefcase. "It's early. We can have him home by dinnertime."

"Bring him to my apartment. I'll feed you both." She paused, smiling slightly. "Correction, Shelby, she's a professional chef, will feed you."

"That's a better gig than jailhouse grub," Devin commented.

"She's probably pacing outside the door by now, so I'm gonna let you two talk." Calla laid her hand over Howard's, then turned and kissed Devin. She lingered longer than anybody ever had in this bleak room. "The gang has your back," she murmured against his cheek.

"You're not a gang," he said automatically.

She grinned as she moved away. "We are now."

When the door closed behind her, Howard was the first to speak. "You know how amazing she is, right?"

"I do."

"Then we'll get along fine."

8

Who Needs Pregnant Pop Stars
When You've Got the NYPD?
by Peeps Galloway, Gossipmonger
(And proud of it!)

Yes, fellow gossip compatriots, it's true. Maybe it was inevitable. I can now take *apparently* out of my report on Detective Devin Antonio. Arrested on assault. Charged and arraigned. Released on bail. It's traumatic, it's, it's…

Delicious.

I mean, you just can't make this stuff up. (And, believe me, I've tried.) I hear he's holed up with his lawyer and his pals—at least the ones who aren't being interrogated—to prepare his defense. In the meantime, the press is going nuts, asking tough questions about dirty cops, protection for average citizens and whether the screening process for the academy ought to be toughened.

But me? I'm asking the *right* questions. Did he

assault his victim because he'd slipped the bartender a twenty so he could get his pomegranate martini right away, only to have said server rebuff him for a C-list TV star he obviously wanted to get naked with? Or maybe his victim cut the line at a shoe sale at Macy's? Or at a designer sample sale? ('Cause any and all are more-than-valid defenses in my book.)

Is he dating that blonde, who *must* have a celebrity highlight expert on speed dial? And, even more importantly, who got the lucky task of strip-searching the sizzling hot cop?

All those questions and more will be answered right here, my lovelies, if you're only patient.

I'm kidding, of course! I'm on it. In fact, I'm going to get an exclusive....

And, yet, there's a hint of melancholy (yes, I know what the word means) in this post. I honestly thought Detective Antonio was one of the good guys.

—*Peeps*

"OUR JAILBIRD IS FREE," Howard said the moment Calla opened her apartment door.

Calla kissed Howard's cheek, told him to make himself comfortable in the living room, then, balancing the kitten beneath her arm, grabbed Devin.

He looked the same, felt the same. But everything had changed. What had they done to him in the past several hours? Even the thought of the humiliation and injustice he'd suffered was beyond anything she could imagine.

"You're wearing another dress," he said.

She glanced down at the poppy-red swing dress,

straight out of the fifties. "I shopped. I got Sharky a proper litter box, some food and a basket to sleep in. Then I saw this in a window. Vintage clothing store plus nervous energy equals charges dismissed."

He absently scratched the cat between his ears. "It's bright."

"After that horribly gray interrogation room, plus— you know—jail, I figured you could use the color."

"They didn't keep me in the regular holding cells."

"Why?"

"They like to kill cops in jail."

She felt the blood drain from her face.

He pulled her against him, where his heart beat steady and strong. A small comfort. "That was supposed to make you smile."

"Yeah. Dying in prison, you're a real comedian."

"I waited in a conference room."

"Oh."

He wrapped his arm around her waist as they headed down the hall. "How long do we have to hang out with Howard?" he said in a low voice. "I was hoping we could be alone."

"I've waited all day to hear the evidence against you. We're due to meet Shelby and Victoria and the guys for dinner." She glanced at her watch. "In less than an hour."

"Then let's get on with this legal stuff." He slid his fingertips down her side. "I have other plans for us."

"Sex?" she whispered, astonished. "You're thinking about sex now?"

"No sympathy? I was in jail."

"You were in a conference room."

He halted. "I shouldn't have told you that."

She shifted her body between him and the living

room, where Howard waited with reality and evidence. "You want sex for comfort, or because you just do?"

"I'm a guy. It's like eggs." He brushed his lips across her cheek. "You have no idea how glad I am to see you."

The emotion in his eyes was like crystal-clear water. "Look how good you are at learning to share."

"Do you have to make me sound like a kindergardener who's learned to use a crayon?"

"Yes, because then we'll get to play."

By the time Calla and Devin walked into the living room, Howard had set up a grease board with pictures and a diagram relating to the case against Devin.

"Is there a slide presentation, too?" Calla asked.

With a bright blue marker in his hand, Howard turned, his puppy-dog brown eyes blinking behind his overlarge frames. "I could boot up the laptop, but I figured you'd want the raw data first."

Calla patted Howard's shoulder before sitting beside Devin on the sofa and settling the cat in her lap. "I was kidding, Howard."

"I've developed this new multimedia software for courtroom presentations." Howard puffed out his skinny chest. "Not every lawyer has the charm I do with juries. I think it's quite effective. Maybe you could give me some pointers?" He smiled. "You know, from a stunningly hot woman's perspective?"

"I haven't seen a stunningly hot woman on a jury in ten years," Devin said, casually laying his arm on the back of the couch behind Calla.

"I'd be glad to give you pointers," Calla said to Howard after throwing Devin a chill-out stare. Possessiveness was flattering, but she wanted to avoid open hostility. They needed Howard.

"So, go ahead, counselor," Devin said, his sarcasm

obvious. "Give her the happy news. It's coming up on cocktail hour, and I have big plans."

Calla scowled. "I don't have whiskey."

"I know a liquor store that delivers."

"Devin, I don't think—"

"Do you want to know the dirty details or not?" he countered.

Calla scoffed. "This whole deal is a crappy frame. Did they find a crumpled piece of paper on your desk with Forrester's name on it? How about a signed confession letter?"

"Not so crappy," Howard said, putting a series of photos on the board.

"They found a pipe with my prints on it," Devin informed her calmly.

"Don't forget about the surveillance photos," Howard added as Calla gasped.

"B-but," Calla sputtered. "How? You didn't hit Forrester. Surely they're bluffing, hoping you'll confess."

"They're not," Howard assured her. "I saw the lab reports."

"Still believe I'm gonna get out of this with my badge?" Devin asked.

Calla slumped against the sofa cushions. "And the photos?"

Howard pointed to the board. "Here's a few. They're basically shots of Jimmie in various low-rent areas of town. All handily saved on a data card in a digital camera obtained via a search on Devin's apartment."

Calla straightened. "They can't just—"

"Seized last night by a warrant," Howard added.

"While you were here." Calla sighed. "I suppose your prints were all over that, too."

Devin shook his head. "No prints on the camera

or data card. Apparently, I had enough sense to wipe them off."

"And leave them on the pipe?" Calla asked incredulously.

"I'm a brilliant cop but a terrible crook." Devin splayed his hands. "Can't have everything."

Calla rubbed her temples, trying to process this latest disaster. "So whoever hit Jimmie and Devin had the sense to wipe off his prints, or wear gloves, then wrap Devin's hand around the pipe while he was unconscious. And last night, sometime after nine, which was when Devin got here, either Jimmie or his accomplice broke into Devin's apartment, planted the camera, then got out again before the NYPD arrived with their search warrant."

"The warrant was signed by Judge Cooper at one-twenty a.m.," Howard said, writing the number on the board and circling it.

"Let me guess," Calla began, disgusted by the whole business. "I'm betting this incredibly convenient instinct to search Devin's apartment was arrived at after the ole standby of an anonymous phone call."

"Brilliant and beautiful," Howard commented, earning a warning glare from Devin. "The NYPD won't say anything about their hunches, but we can assume an outside tip was involved."

"Unless the evidence fairy makes house calls," Devin said sardonically. "We can also assume my apartment was being watched by Jimmie and/or his pal."

"If only we'd stayed at your place," Calla murmured, gliding her fingers over Devin's clenched fist.

"My fault," he reminded her.

As he stood and walked away from her, Calla tried not to take his distance personally. The full weight of everything they faced was only now becoming apparent. Someone had planned this attack against Devin very, very, carefully. And with the bad guys several steps ahead, the gang had to anticipate their next moves if they were going to clear Devin's name and get him reinstated.

"If they're watching your apartment, then we should be watching them," she suggested.

Devin shook his head. "Fake evidence mission accomplished. Why would they keep up the surveillance?"

"Any ideas, Howard?" she asked, feeling useless. She was way out of her element here.

"Nothing concrete. I'd like to go over the time and date stamp in the digital photos and compile a time line. Maybe some of them are old, or we can prove Devin was somewhere else when a certain picture was taken."

Devin looked impressed. "That's good. Send me the images, and I'll go through them on Calla's computer."

"Dinner, remember?" Calla crossed her arms over her chest and tried to look stern. Easy enough, she copied Devin's usual expression. "You need to relax and be with friends. After a good night's sleep, things will look much clearer."

Devin's gaze held hers. Not that they'd gotten much sleep last night....

Calla cleared her throat as she directed her attention to Howard. "Shelby's place is in Chelsea, and we can discuss Devin's case while we eat."

Howard crossed to her, captured her hand and brushed his lips over the back. "Not tonight, my lovely. Why don't I make a slide presentation of the photos in chronological order, then we'll meet at my office at ten tomorrow and review Devin's movements during?"

"Do you two mind if I have a vote in my own life?" Devin asked, clearly annoyed.

"Yes!" Calla and Howard announced together as Howard helped Calla to her feet.

Devin pulled Calla's hand away from the lawyer. "I guess this is good-night, then."

They helped Howard with his board and supplies, then fed Sharky and got him settled in his new basket. After Calla gave the cabbie Trevor and Shelby's address, Devin told her, "We need to make a stop first."

"We don't. Trevor has better booze than either of us could ever afford." She laid her hand on his thigh. "Don't you think you should stay sharp so we can brainstorm your defense?"

"Howard has everything under control. You were right, I need to relax. Tonight that means a good meal, a smooth drink and you."

Not too long ago she would have considered a statement like that from him as a delusional fantasy. Maybe he was using her as a crutch to get him through these terrible events, but she was happy to support him regardless.

"Who knows how many nights of freedom I have left?" Devin added.

"Don't kid about stuff like that. You have plenty." She laid her head on his shoulder as he slipped his arm around her waist. "The gang and I, plus Howard, are all behind you."

"My instinct is to be alone, you know."

"I know."

"Tonight, though, I'm happy to be your plus-one. What's for dinner?"

"With Shelby in charge, it's gotta be something good.

And you're not an afterthought of this gathering. You're the guest of honor."

"That's what I'm worried about. There are some rampant pair-ups going on in your gang."

"If you're imagining a shotgun wedding, you'll have to wait till my dad comes back to town."

"Thanks for the tip. Escaping to Texas may be my last option. Think I'd look good in a Stetson?"

"I've never seen you look bad in anything, so, yeah, but I don't think you'd like Texas."

"Why's that?"

"Because they don't just kill corrupt cops in Texas, they torture them and bury their bodies in the desert."

"That's not funny."

"Maybe just a little funny."

As the cab pulled to the curb in front of Shelby's luxury high-rise apartment, Devin handed the driver the fare through the window. He didn't speak again until they'd been cleared through security and were riding up in the elevator. "Why don't you doubt me? There've been moments the last few days that even I've wondered if I caught Jimmie in that alley, beat him up then somehow blocked it out. But your belief in me hasn't wavered. Why not?"

"It's not logical," she said. "You certainly didn't hit yourself."

"Nothing more than common sense?"

She stroked his cheek with the tip of her finger. "I see the best in you."

"Can't be easy," he muttered.

Laughing, Calla linked arms with him as they exited the elevator and headed down the hall. Shelby and Trevor's apartment was contemporary luxury, with modern decor of steel, glass and marble, and spectacular views of the Manhattan skyline.

Since Trevor owned a multimillion-dollar transportation company—not to mention his father was an English earl—the address and size of their place was expected. And though Shelby's upbringing and income were a lot more modest, she'd added love and warmth, so the space suited them both.

And it was a great clubhouse for the gang.

Victoria opened the door. "You made the local news."

Devin groaned. "And the fun just keeps on comin'."

"Trevor's got a special get-out-of-jail drink waiting for you at the bar," Victoria said, extending her arm in welcome.

As Devin headed down the hall, Victoria pulled Calla close for a rare show of physical affection. "How ya holding up, Polly?"

"I'm still standing."

Her light blue gaze scanned Calla's outfit. "You sort of look like a Stepford wife."

"That's how I'm holding up."

By the time she reached the living area, Devin was holding a crystal tumbler in his hand standing in front of the windows with his back to the room.

Over the past few months, she'd been by often to see Shelby and brought dates to dinner parties here, but Devin hadn't visited since Labor Day, when they'd all shared a barbecue to celebrate another triumph for Robin Hood and his crew.

Was he glad to be welcomed back, or wary of being the center of attention?

The latter, definitely.

Turning from him, she greeted her friends and got a big, lifted-off-her-feet hug from Victoria's boyfriend,

Jared, who she hadn't seen since the wedding, as he'd been leading a scuba diving adventure to Maui.

"You're tan," she commented as he set her down.

"You look like you could use one," he returned.

"Book me on your next tour," she said dryly. "I could use a little excitement in my life."

Shelby pressed a glass of wine into her hand, and Calla relaxed for the first time all day. With her friends by her side, there was nothing they couldn't do.

She received a kiss on the cheek from Trevor, who was elegantly dressed, as always, in navy pants and a pristine white shirt.

Devin got miffed whenever Howard smiled at her. Why wasn't he jumping in the middle of two gorgeous men kissing and hugging her? Granted, they were deeply in love with her two best friends, but still....

Glancing at him, she noticed he *had* noticed her, after all. The ever-present scowl was back.

"How's the whiskey?" Trevor asked lightly, making Calla wonder if he understood the reason for Devin's sour expression.

After only a slight hesitation, he approached the group. "Perfect. Thanks."

"Do you feel like talking about the case against you?" Trevor asked. "We'd like to help."

"Calla tells it better," Devin said.

So Calla told it.

Everybody agreed the frame-up was obvious to anybody who knew Devin, but they also agreed untangling the tricked-up evidence, identifying Jimmie's partner and especially the *why* of it all, was going to be challenging.

"I find it hard to believe the D.A. can bring a decent case," Trevor commented. "The evidence is inconsistent, and there's absolutely no motive. Why are they saying Devin suddenly decided to stalk and later assault a small-time thief with a mental condition?"

"Bad cops are bad press for the NYPD," Victoria said. "Allegedly bad cops in this case."

"So it's better one of their officers is arrested?" Obviously baffled, Trevor shook his head. "Bad strategy."

"We've arrested regular people with less evidence," Devin pointed out.

"I'm with Trevor," Shelby said firmly. "Officials would win more support in the long run standing by their top cops."

Devin set aside his glass. "My lieutenant does—as much as he can, anyway. He thinks my arrest might make the real culprits relax."

"Which would be great if he was running the investigation," Calla reminded him. "Instead, there's stoic Colin Reid and IAB."

"Leaving us to prove Devin's innocence," Jared concluded.

Victoria sipped her wine. "We have experience chasing guilty people. Think we can reverse the procedure?"

"I don't see why not." Shelby rose. "For now, though, we eat. How does everybody feel about steak?"

Devin's eyes lit as they did when he was aroused, and Calla felt an answering response deep in her belly. "Much better than I do about clearing my record."

While Shelby put the steaks on the grill, everybody else helped in the kitchen or with setting the table. Devin's case wasn't mentioned the rest of the night. He relaxed and even laughed, and Calla silently swore she'd keep that optimism alive, no matter what she had to do.

She'd helped Shelby and Victoria with their recent troubles and understood their need to relieve their heartache, but she hadn't fully realized the depths of their determination until now. She hadn't grasped the lengths to which they'd undoubtedly been willing to go to deliver justice.

In or outside the law.

As she and Devin got into a cab in front of the apartment building, he grasped her hand. "Will you come home with me?"

Flustered by the direct question, she managed only a nod.

"I want to check out my place," he said after giving the cabbie the address. "See where Reid and his boys snooped. My gun safe for one."

"I thought you left your gun at my apartment when you went to the station."

"I did. Dark blue shoe box, gold lettering."

The blood drained from her face. "The Stuart Weitzmans? How could you—" She narrowed her eyes. "Wait. You want me in your apartment so we can see what the NYPD poked into?"

"You have a good eye." He trailed his finger down her throat. "Plus I have this thing about you in my bed."

"This thing?"

"Vision. Fantasy. Delusion, possibly," he added quickly when she didn't respond.

She leaned close, stopping less than an inch from his lips. "Fantasy works. Are there costumes, sets and scripts?"

He slid his hand around her head, tangling his fingers in her hair. "No clothing needed, the bed works for me and you don't have to say a word except *yes*."

She smiled. "The zipper on this dress sticks a bit."

When he slammed his apartment door closed behind them, he quickly discovered the truth of her statement.

He solved the problem with quick action, ripping the zipper down the seam, while simultaneously muttering a promise to have it fixed.

He pushed her dress past her hips, and she tossed his T-shirt on the floor as they crossed the threshold of the bedroom doorway. Indulging in his pumping heat, she wrapped her arms around his neck, trailing her lips across his skin.

His enticing scent, inviting and masculine, spun her wits and intensified the hunger building inside. After the turmoil of the day, she craved his touch. When his hands cupped her breasts, she let her head fall back on a moan.

He pressed her to the bed, never ceasing his caress. He let go of her only long enough to strip off the rest of his clothes, while she did the same with hers, then he was hovering over her.

"I don't deserve you, but I'm taking you, anyway," he mumbled against her lips.

As his mouth captured hers and their bodies became one, her heart hammered in her chest, her need spiraled. She hooked her legs around his hips when he surged inside.

Tingles raced down her spine, and her joy only increased as she saw the pleasure stamped on his face. Delight built on delight, tightening her muscles, driving her higher. His strokes quickened. Her breath caught as she reached the peak, and pulses of satisfaction rippled through her.

As he followed her over the edge, a fission of fear spoiled her bliss. He needed her so much now, but would he need her, and want her, when he had his life back?

9

PARKED AT THE CURB IN front of a convenience mart and a bakery on the Lower East Side, Devin stared at the dingy apartment building out his left window. "There's something really wrong about sitting in a Mercedes and eating gourmet food while spying on a low-life thief."

"I'm not sure what," Calla returned, holding a cracker in front of his face. "Shelby's curried chicken salad never disappoints."

"It's supposed to be bad coffee and street-corner hot dogs," he muttered, though he took the cracker. "My life has changed in remarkable ways since meeting you."

She pressed her lips to his cheek. "All in a good way."

Good didn't even begin to cover his life lately. Remarkable, miraculous…perilous—those were better descriptions.

Calla was devoted to him. After the dinner party at the Banfields', they'd spent all night and most of the next day in his bed. She was adventurous, interesting, curious and joyful. He'd never known anyone like her.

"How does Jimmie afford this place?" he wondered aloud, hoping to get his mind back on his mission. "Even a dump is out of his income bracket."

"Maybe he's a better thief than you think."

"Or maybe his partner is well financed."

"You're sure your friend at the station is reliable? Reid could have told him to lie to you, trying to keep you off the case."

"Reid doesn't know about your gang."

She handed him another cracker piled with chicken salad. "But I bet he knows everything about you, so he'd realize you won't sit around stroking a rosary while waiting for your trial to start."

The image of a pious him made him choke on his snack.

Calla whacked him on the back. "If you stop breathing, can I give you mouth-to-mouth?"

Clearing his throat, he scooped her off her seat and into his lap. "Absolutely."

She raised her eyebrows. "Do you usually make out during stakeouts?"

"Never." He gave her a long, slow kiss that got his blood pumping way more than any department operation ever had. "Especially on Sunday night. Nothing happens on Sunday night."

"Why not?"

He trailed his lips across her jaw. Vanilla wafted from her hair. He threaded his fingers though the golden silk. "Bad guys take the night off, I guess. Maybe they're spending quality time with their rosaries. How do you always smell so amazing?"

"One of those girly gifts. Speaking of girls, this woman from your past, the stabbing smuggler who seduced you, what was she like?"

He stilled. "That was an interesting segue."

"I was kind of hoping to catch you off guard and you'd blurt something out."

Saying nothing, he stared at her.

"Right. You're not much of a blurter." She traced his lips with her finger. "Any chance of telling me, anyway?"

"She was beautiful, quick-thinking and cold."

She tensed. "How beautiful?"

"Very. She looked like you."

"You're comparing me to a murderess?" she asked in disbelief.

"Superficially."

"Why'd you want to know?" He cocked his head. "Jealous?"

"Since she's doing twenty-five to life, I don't think I'll have to arm-wrestle her for you."

"How about wrestling in bikinis?"

"Men are such degenerates. So the fact that she and I look alike didn't have anything to do with why you refused to trust me and kept me at a snarly distance for six months?"

Years of experience kept his expression neutral.

Which didn't fool her for a second.

Her expression froze. "You think I'm going to betray you?"

"No."

She moved back to her seat. "Not anymore," she corrected.

"Not ever." He leaned over, bracketing her. "You're the exact opposite of her. But the fact that she fooled me is absolute proof that I have no idea what I'm doing when it comes to personal relationships. You deserve more."

"So you said the other night. What's changed?"

"Everything. Our proximity, you saving me. I couldn't stop myself anymore. Still can't. And though

I might not have given in to my attraction to you before last week, I dreamed about you constantly."

Her gaze held his. "Day and night?"

"Yes."

"You *did* send the text."

"Yes."

"You said you didn't."

"I was wary. I was afraid admitting the truth would lead to us getting together."

"Which you didn't want."

"Which I *thought* I didn't want. The last two nights proved pretty conclusively that I want you very much."

Looking wary herself, Calla licked her lips. "Do you think our attraction has anything to do with your career and freedom being in jeopardy?"

"It was there before all this happened. I guess it'll be there afterward."

"I'm not asking for commitments or promises."

"Especially since I could be in prison soon."

She laid her finger over his lips. "Don't talk like that. I don't want to be merely a distraction."

She'd asked for nothing in this deal with him, but she'd given everything. Though he didn't express his feelings well, he had to find a way to show her how vital her support and understanding had been. "You're all that gives me hope. I only know how to be a cop. If I don't have that, I'm nothing."

"I don't agree, but thanks. We're going to get you through this."

He rested his forehead against hers, soaking up the comfort of her words and her touch. "Do I get a gang nickname?"

"You can be the sheriff."

He frowned. "I thought he was the bad guy. The corrupt lawman, in fact."

Her lips turned up at the corners in a sly smile. "What do you know about Robin Hood?"

"Enough. Wasn't there a king?"

"Richard. But he was off on a crusade or fighting a battle or something, which is why the whole mess with the crooked sheriff happened in the first place. You're the star of this show, so you can't be him."

"Okay, then I get to be Robin."

"I'm Robin."

"Who says?"

"Everybody. Shelby and Victoria got to be Robin when it was their turn. I think there was a marksman. You can be him. Luigi Greeneyes."

"His name was Will Scarlet."

Calla got that adamant look in her eyes, the one he used to run from whenever he saw it aimed in his direction. "I'm the gang leader. I get to pick the names."

"Why Luigi?"

"It's Italian, of course. And it means warrior, or something like that. I'll have to look it up."

As she reached into her purse for her phone, he heard a noise outside the car. "Quiet," he ordered, reaching beneath his jacket for the pistol holstered against his side.

Calla immediately slumped in her seat and tucked her phone, with its glowing screen, behind her back. She said nothing, but she clenched the door handle.

A few seconds later, a man and a woman, their arms around each other walked under the streetlight in front of Jimmie's building. They were laughing and stumbling a bit. They paused at the corner and indulged in an energetic kiss.

At least somebody's Sunday night was eventful.

When they moved up the stairs, Devin holstered his weapon. "I doubt either one of them is our accomplice."

"Agreed."

After sighting the couple, several more possible residents or visitors entered the building. But the collection included a slow-moving elderly couple and two sets of parents with children. No single male entered, no one who looked furtive or out of place, and no one came back out.

Just after midnight, when they were confident their mission had been a big waste of time, a cab stopped at the far end of the block, and a figure emerged. Heading toward them, and Jimmie's building, the person was dressed in black or dark blue and moved with brisk purpose, looking left and right as they moved.

Not suspiciously, really. Any wise-thinking New Yorker wore dark clothes and was aware of their surroundings at night on a deserted street.

"It's a woman," Devin said as the person grew closer.

"There's definitely a hip sway when she walks," Calla agreed. "Could Jimmie's partner be a woman?"

"I guess." Though he'd assumed a man simply because of the violent nature of the crime. Detectives should gather facts, not assume. But if a woman had whacked both him and Jimmie, neither one of them would ever live it down. "It's not like I can go charging in there and ask him."

The woman had a key to the outer door, and she managed to avoid the light on the stoop before disappearing inside.

"I couldn't see her face," Calla said.

"She kept it turned away."

"On purpose?"

He shrugged. Something about her seemed off, but

he wasn't sure what. Could be wishful thinking—he wanted something significant to happen, so he was putting too much emphasis on her.

A few other people went in, but still no single male appeared, and no one else gave him a tingle at the the back of his neck.

He and Calla ate, talked and drank coffee. She dozed after a while, arranging a pillow she'd brought, laying her head in his lap. He absently stroked her hair and chased away the image of her visiting him from behind bulletproof glass while he wore prison orange.

But then that would never happen.

He'd never let her see him that way.

Leaning his head against the window, he stared blankly toward Jimmie's building. Investigating was different when the case was personal. Impartiality was nonexistent, the stakes were higher, and concentration was tougher.

Fear kept him off balance. He kept wondering if his time was limited, if he should have appreciated his badge more when he'd had it in his pocket. He continually second-guessed himself, considering which move would sink him, and which one might be his salvation. Since his gut instincts and decisiveness were some of his most valuable assets, the uncertainty was a major problem.

As he yawned, he thought about the comfort of his bed, or Calla's. They'd left the cat with food and his basket. She'd even convinced him to add a heating pad beneath his blankets, so he'd feel warm and secure. Still, Sharky had glared as they left, as if he'd known they were leaving for a long time, like they had after the dinner party at the Banfields'.

Last night Calla had jolted upright in his bed, then

dragged them both over to her place to pick him up so Sharky wouldn't be alone all night. Devin expected she'd wake up any second and remind him their tiny bundle of joy was lonely. Maybe they should buy some catnip or a toy on the way home. At least he'd drawn the line at bringing a kitten on a stakeout....

A loud rap on the car window woke Devin from a dead sleep.

Blinking, he noted dawn was breaking and Lieutenant Meyer's angry face greeted him from the other side of the glass. "Out of the car, Antonio."

He did as ordered, easing his way out of the car, so he hopefully wouldn't wake up Calla. "I know I shouldn't be here, sir," he began, hoping his brain would kick in a reasonable excuse for being outside Jimmie's apartment building. "But it's my badge on the line, and I had to see what Jimmie was up to. I didn't hit him, and I'm pretty certain he didn't hit me, so somebody else is involved in—"

"Why are you at my crime scene?"

Devin's attention shifted from Meyer's fury to the area around him. Two patrol cars, barricades, somber expressions, uniforms talking to people milling around the apartment building. "What crime scene? What's going on?"

"Jimmie Forrester is dead."

"I ABSOLUTELY WOULDN'T believe it if I hadn't witnessed the scene with my own eyes," Lieutenant Meyer ranted, pacing his office as Calla and Devin sat stiffly in the guest chairs.

Technically, Meyer couldn't question Devin before his lawyer arrived—though that hadn't stopped him from ordering them inside, drawing the blinds and yelling off his frustration at finding them smack in the middle of Jimmie's murder site.

An *alleged* murder, anyway. According to the medics, Jimmie had died of a drug overdose in the early morning hours Monday. Jimmie supposedly didn't do recreational drugs, as he already had several legit prescriptions to combat his mental health issues.

But since the cops had found *alleged* evidence against Devin at both the assault in the alley and in his apartment, Calla was holding off on buying into Jimmie's Just Say No lifestyle.

"In a little over a week, you're found unconscious at *two* crime scenes," Meyer continued, his voice as frigidly terse as Calla's dad's had been when he'd found out she was secretly dating bad boy Clint Hampton in the tenth grade. "The odds are...well, there are no odds. It's incalculable!"

"Exactly, sir," Devin said, his voice much stronger than Calla's had been her sophomore year. "That's because I was outside Jimmie's place on purpose last night. I'm accused of assault. I can't sit around and wait for Reid to use me to get his captain's bars."

"Reid's a good man," Meyer asserted.

"But he's wrong about me," Devin returned.

"You were *armed*." Meyer lifted his hands to the ceiling, as if divine intervention might work its way down somehow. "You can't carry a gun in the city while you're on suspension."

Devin coolheadedly met his boss's fury. "Sir, I can explain—"

"It's my gun," Calla burst out. "Devin was holding it for me," she added lamely.

Meyer braced his hand on the back of her chair and

pushed his face inches from hers. "And how do you have a permit to carry a concealed weapon?"

She didn't, of course. But she was pretty handy with computer graphics. Maybe she could forge a—

"You don't," Meyer argued before she could think of a reasonable lie.

Calla would've loved to have the comfort of Devin's hand in hers, but as her lover's hands were currently clenching the arms of his chair so tightly his knuckles were white, she instead hoped Howard's cab wasn't stuck in traffic. "But I do have a theory," she said, hoping her voice didn't crack. "A drug overdose is like poison, right? And women are more likely to be poisoners. Well, we saw a woman outside Jimmie's apartment last night, so—"

"Remind me again when you graduated from the police academy," Meyer shot back.

"Sir, please." Devin rose, moving between his boss and Calla. "She's the only one who believes me."

"Plus, I'm his alibi." Calla pushed herself to stand. And not behind Devin, either. Though her knees wobbled, she forced herself to meet Meyer's gaze. "Devin has been with me since Friday night."

"As I recall," Meyer said, his tone clipped, "you were asleep when I got to Jimmie's."

On the verge of her own rant, Calla held back a scream of frustration. "So you think Devin snuck out while I was sleeping and killed Jimmie?"

"No, but he *could* have. Motive, means, opportunity." Meyer ticked the points off on his fingers. "It's all there."

This was beyond ridiculous. Calla couldn't imagine crimes were actually solved with this kind of logic. "You honestly believe Devin and I ordered a picnic dinner, picked it up from my best friend's catering company, borrowed my other best friend's Mercedes, parked across from Jimmie's apartment building, waited until the coast was clear, snuck in, murdered him with some icky needle thing, then slipped back into the car and fell asleep while waiting for you and your blue lights to show up?"

Meyer seemed stunned into silence.

Devin's mouth twisted into a smirk. "Her succinctness is only one of her many amazing qualities."

"I'm also stubborn as hell." Calla crossed her arms over her chest. "If anything, you cops should be dancing around the Maypole. This latest frame-up proves Devin—who's one of your own, if you might call—is innocent."

"Maypole?" Meyer echoed. "Is she for real?" he asked Devin.

"She's from Texas."

"There are procedures, Ms. Tucker," Meyer explained with barely restrained exasperation. "You and Devin were found mere yards from the scene of a suspicious death, the living quarters, by the way, of the star witness against him. Without Jimmie to testify, it's likely the assault case will be dismissed."

Calla looked surprised. *"Really?"* she questioned mockingly. "I didn't realize you needed Jimmie. I thought you had other bogus evidence to fall back on."

Meyer wasn't impressed with her sarcasm. "We do. Evidence that can be rolled over into Devin's murder trial."

"Uh-huh. And we're sure it's murder because poor, sweet Jimmie would never do drugs." She tapped her finger against her chin, pretending to contemplate. "He'd just frame a cop for assault."

For a second, Meyer seemed as though he might smile, but the impulse passed as he walked stiffly around his desk. "Despite the appearance that I'm blind and deaf, I know there's more to this than where the circumstances point. But, as cops, we have to follow the evidence."

Calla glared at him. "Well, I think the whole case is stupid."

"Unfortunately, law enforcement doesn't get to decide that. Juries do." Meyer shifted his stare to Devin. "Typically, you've said little, Detective. I imagine you're regretting your rogue investigation about now."

"No way." Devin sent Calla a grateful glance. "In fact, I'm stepping up my efforts. Whoever's behind this is way more dangerous than any of us thought. The sooner he—or she—is behind bars, the safer we'll all be."

Calla gave his hand a supportive squeeze. "Spoken like a true cop."

"I figured as much." Meyer scooped up Devin's pistol, dangling it by the butt before shoving it in his desk drawer. "Which is why I'm keeping this. You're lucky I don't charge you with possession."

"I need to protect myself," Devin said, his vivid green eyes glaring. "And those around me."

"Stay away from this case, and you won't need to." Meyer collapsed in his chair, probably knowing Devin wouldn't follow his order.

Calla thought about bringing up the obvious point that Devin had a gun on hand, so he wouldn't have needed to kill Jimmie with drugs. Meyer would probably point out that the gun could have been used to keep Jimmie under control while the lethal dose was administered.

It seemed everything about this investigation could be interpreted in a variety of ways. And there was almost too much information. A muddle of motives and contradictory evidence that slithered around the system, popping up to cause frustration, confusion, divided loyalties and a media explosion.

Almost amateurish, but not quite.

Because it was also crafty and cold-blooded. Frosty enough that one of the assumed conspirators was lying on a slab in the morgue.

"Do you two honestly think your presence was part of the frame?" Meyer asked. "That Jimmie's killer knew you were on scene?"

"I don't see how," Devin said. "Only a few friends knew what we were doing. But whoever's behind this knew I'd be the prime suspect regardless. Calla and I being there was a happy accident."

"Happy, huh?" Meyer shook his head in disbelief. "How?"

Looking resolved, Devin rose. "Like Calla said, my killing him and hanging around to wait for the cops is stupid. Jimmie's accomplice—and likely murderer—didn't know we were there last night."

Meyer tapped his pen against his desk. "Dumb moves aside, the setup is getting the job done. Question is, how?"

"And why," Calla added.

Howard, all infuriated ninety-eight pounds of him, burst through the door. "This conversation is over."

Despite her suspicion that the NYPD was holding back and Meyer might have been on the verge of agreeing with them, Calla was wildly glad to see the attorney.

She'd had enough of a scolding for today. She needed to confer with her peeps and figure out what to do next.

She refused to even consider the possibility that Devin could be charged with a crime much worse than assault.

Howard set his briefcase on Meyer's desk—a feat in itself as it was possible the bag weighed more than he did—then flicked his thumbs over the latches. "My recorder is engaged as of this moment."

So saying, Howard removed a tiny, plastic square from his briefcase, which he set on the lieutenant's desk.

Calla, Devin and Meyer all hovered over the device, which was smaller than a stamp. "What is that?" Meyer asked.

Howard snapped his briefcase closed and set it on the floor. "A recording device."

"From an episode of *Star Trek?*" Calla wondered aloud.

Howard smiled before he cleared his throat and resumed a sober expression. "I dabble in electronics."

"Yeah." Calla straightened, looking at Howard with new eyes. "I guess so."

Howard recited the time, date and location, apparently for the benefit of the recorder.

Calla raised her eyebrows. "What? No video capabilities on your alien technology?"

Howard's eyes gleamed. "If the FBI would only let me in their lab…"

Oh, yeah. He was exactly what they needed.

Howard clasped his hands together and turned his attention to Meyer. "Surely you're not questioning my client without his attorney present, Lieutenant? It would be a shame to have to file a civil case against the city after you're forced to apologize to Detective Antonio for falsely accusing him in the first place." Howard pulled his phone from his coat pocket. "I wonder if I still have Channel One on speed dial?"

"Told you he was good," Calla said, winking at Devin.

"I haven't questioned the lieutenant," Meyer said, leaning back in his chair. "I've simply been holding him and Ms. Tucker here until you arrived."

"We appreciate your consideration," Howard returned. "Somebody's setting up my client. I expect the NYPD is making an effort to find out who."

"I can't comment on an ongoing investigation, but this latest development has everybody's strict attention. Devin Antonio has been a valuable asset to the department for several years, and the investigation surrounding Jimmie Forrester's assault and now death will be given the highest priority."

"Turn off the recording, Howard," Devin ordered.

"Detective, we should—"

"Off," Devin repeated. Once Howard had done so, Devin looked toward Meyer. "We could work together."

"I can't authorize that," Meyer said, his voice clipped.

"We need to go through my old cases and figure out who might be behind all this," Devin continued, undeterred.

Meyer's gaze darted to Calla, no doubt remembering she'd had access to those files for over a week. "Haven't you already?"

Devin shook his head. "Not with an eye toward Jimmie's death—and the woman we saw go into his apartment building."

"The alleged—" Meyer began, only to have the ringing phone interrupt. After a brief conversation, he hung up with a jerky roll of his shoulders. "Lieutenant Reid will meet you in interrogation room two. You can't be there, Ms. Tucker," he added in warning.

Calla slid her arm around Devin. She didn't want to leave him, but she knew Howard was the one to send into the ring and continue the fight. "No worries. I have plenty to do."

Meyer tapped a pen against his desk. "Off the record, I believe you, Detective. I don't think you're responsible for Jimmie's assault or his death. But I can't help you."

Devin said nothing. Howard picked up his briefcase.

Calla kissed Devin's cheek. "Until further notice, he's the sheriff," she muttered before scooting from the room.

10

"THE CITY IMPOUND LOT is probably in Jersey."

Calla understood Victoria's disgust about the events of the morning, but her car's fate wasn't in the top twenty. With her mocha latte and the familiar surroundings of Javalicious to soothe her ragged nerves, she hoped she could hold herself together.

"If I find one scratch," Victoria continued, "I'm suing the city for damages."

Calla dug deep for patience. "Seriously, V, scratches on your eighty-thousand-dollar Mercedes are not a top priority."

Shelby scowled. "Did she equate eighty grand to low priority?"

Looking triumphant, Victoria set her coffee mug on the table. "Yep."

"Hell," Shelby groaned. "She's in love."

"Told you." Victoria held out her hand. "Twenty bucks."

Sometimes her friends were downright maddening. They were supposed to be brainstorming Devin's case.

"If I was in love," Calla began in a stern tone, "the only man who's even remotely a candidate is likely being interrogated for murder. Do you think we can stay on topic here?"

Victoria stuffed her bet winnings in her handbag. "We can multitask. We're women, after all."

"You sure you don't want to talk about your relationship with Devin?" Shelby asked.

"I'm sure." Calla frowned. "I need to concentrate on helping him get his badge back and these charges dismissed before I can even consider anything else."

And that was as good a reason to avoid talking about the amazing, confusing joy she shared with Devin, and its precarious position in her life, as any.

Shelby nodded. "Devin has helped us out plenty of times. It's our turn to be there for him."

"This isn't about payback or friendship for Calla," Victoria insisted.

As much as Calla appreciated Victoria's insight, she wasn't ready for that conversation. Her friends were too good at reading her, and her feelings were too scary to examine. Whoever said *ignorance is bliss* was right on the money. "It is today."

Calla's stubbornness was matched by few people, and since Victoria was one of those, she was surprised when her friend said, "So we're looking for a woman."

Shelby's eyes darkened with worry. "A killer."

"Not necessarily," Calla said. "Maybe Jimmie really did overdose. Devin described him as jittery. The police say he's mentally unstable. He could have taken the drug on this own."

"Suicide?" Victoria wondered.

Calla still found it hard to believe things had gotten so grave in less than twenty-four hours. "That can't be ruled out, I guess."

"But Meyer thinks it was murder," Shelby prompted.

"He used words like *alleged* and *suspicious death,* but, yeah, I think so." Calla recalled the lieutenant's anger and concern. This turn in the case had thrown him, too. "Until the autopsy is finished, we can't know for sure."

"When will that be?" Victoria asked.

"Sometime today, I guess," Calla said. "Not that Reid is likely to tell us the results. And Devin's contact who's been feeding us information at the precinct is in robbery. I don't know if he can find out anything about a possible murder."

"Regardless," Shelby put in, "we need to go through Devin's case files to find a woman."

"Not necessarily a woman he arrested, though." Victoria cupped her hands around her mug. "Somebody's wife or sister, somebody pissed off her loved one was arrested."

Calla considered the new angle Victoria had proposed. It was one option among so many. She wasn't sure which tactic would yield the best results, and the continual images of Devin in that stark interrogation room weren't helping. If Howard wasn't with him, she didn't see how she wouldn't melt into a useless puddle on the floor. "The woman could also be a cousin, maiden aunt or college roommate. The possibilities are endless. It's a daunting task."

Shelby sighed. "Especially without our usual inside source—Devin."

"He'll be around later," Calla said, hoping she sounded more confident than she felt.

"Sure he will." Shelby sipped her cappuccino, probably to hide worry lines. "I can't believe Lieutenant Meyer won't help."

Victoria leaned back in her chair. "He doesn't want internal affairs knocking on his door, too."

"He's as worried as we are." Though Calla was disappointed he wouldn't do more. "Devin worked with a homicide cop back in the spring. Maybe he'd be willing to give us the inside scoop."

"It's worth a try," Shelby agreed.

Whether it was the coffee or the familiarity, Calla already felt better. "I'll get Devin to contact him while we—"

Victoria's phone chimed. "Sorry, that's the alarm for my meeting."

"Thanks, guys." Calla stood and hugged each of her friends. "I appreciate you taking the time."

"Meet later to go over the case files?" Victoria asked.

Calla found a smile. "You bet. You still need to meet Sharky."

"The cat?" Victoria wrinkled her nose. "Guess I won't wear black."

Shelby gave Victoria an affectionately exasperated look. "I'm sure he's adorable."

As Calla rode the subway back to her apartment, she was surprised how eagerly she was looking forward to seeing her *adorable* new addition. Once she'd buried her face in his soft fur, apologized for dumping him while she raced off to a stakeout, she was sure she could pull out her laptop and concentrate on research.

She wouldn't think about Devin's meeting with Reid, the shaky state of the bond with her new lover or the possibility of anything going wrong with the investigation.

When she walked inside and called Sharky's name, she got no response. She guessed cats weren't the overly communicative type. She found him sitting on the coffee table, his long, furry tail dangling over the side, his green eyes glaring in her direction.

"I know, I know," she said in apology. "I was out all night, but I thought you'd be more comfortable here than at Devin's. I left you plenty of food."

Sharky's tail twitched.

"I know you like fresh tuna. I promise to go by the market before dinner."

Sharky's ears twitched.

Bribery wasn't working. It was time for a distraction. Dumping her purse on the counter, she snagged his mouse toy. Approaching him, she dangled it just out of reach.

His eyes gleamed.

Aha.

After a few minutes of keep-away and a few belly scratches, she and Sharky were back in sync. He napped on the arm of her chair while she worked on her laptop.

Devin had the files, but she didn't want them anyway. She wanted to concentrate on him, the cases he'd been involved in that had gotten press. The big ones.

She called a friend at a local newspaper, another who was a nurse at the hospital, a contact in the deputy D.A.'s office. She made pages of notes, considered motives and tried to think logically, instead of emotionally. Considering the subject was Devin, the challenge was extensive.

After several hours, she felt she was finally getting somewhere.

She was convinced Jimmie's partner was a woman

who'd been using him to get to Devin. Someone she loved had been arrested by him.

Wait. Not only arrested. *Wronged*.

Hadn't Calla and her friends gotten into their Robin Hood adventures for the same reason? Either they or somebody they cared about had been a victim of someone more powerful or clever.

They hadn't hesitated to do whatever they had to in order to right the wrong. This plan was more extreme, but it had eerily similar echoes.

The steps had been considered in advance. All the consequences accounted for. The mastermind had gotten Jimmie to lure Devin into chasing him. She'd knocked out Devin, then beat up Jimmie. When Devin was arrested for Jimmie's assault, she'd eliminated her co-conspirator.

She imagined Jimmie had been definitely surprised by that part of the plan.

Either by design or inexperience, she'd set up the confusing clues. Beating that pointed to a man, poisoning—that indicated a woman; prints on the pipe, the camera wiped clean.

Jimmie was unstable, recently released from prison and lonely. He'd be easy prey for a woman set on vengeance.

Those were the steps. Laid out as she saw them.

Cold revenge. Calla had felt it from the beginning, and she was becoming convinced she was right to listen to those instincts.

The police were taught to gather evidence, follow its path and not pre-judge. Maybe that was true, and maybe it wasn't, but she wasn't a cop. A lighted trail was flickering on in front of her, and she was walking that road until somebody could find a way to disprove her theory.

All she knew for certain, though, was that this woman, whoever she might be, was very dangerous.

Can you come over? And bring Sharky.

DEVIN HAD SENT THE message, and Calla had promised she'd come.

Standing in his living room, which Shelby and Victoria had transformed with an intimate table for two, candlelight, a white tablecloth, china, crystal and silver, he slid his hands into his pockets. He didn't know how to charm and impress a woman like Calla, much as he was trying.

Not being indicted for assault could help, he supposed, but once the turmoil in his life subsided, would she hang around for him? He was work-obsessed, moody and uncommunicative.

As she'd already pointed out, he couldn't change his genes or the volatile way he was raised, but could he change a lifetime of resisting intimacy? Could he be who she wanted? Who she needed?

She was both dangerous, and the greatest blessing he could fathom.

For the first time in many years, he was scared. He'd never given his heart to anybody and had no idea how to go about it, or how to recover if everything went wrong.

As jazz echoed through the apartment, he walked around the table, unnecessarily straightening a fork. A fancy salad, plus a chicken and pasta dish, which Shelby had made, sat on the counter, waiting to be served. A high-priced wine, which Victoria had brought, had been submerged into an ice bucket.

So many candles flickered around the room, he was tempted to keep a fire extinguisher nearby, though

Calla's friends had assured him she'd appreciate the effort.

He didn't believe for a second their relationship was as simple as candlelight dancing across crystal, but he was buying the idea for the night. He was holding tight to Calla with both hands.

Howard had been clear about the consequences he faced. Though his lawyer believed events wouldn't progress that far, the hazard that he could go to jail hung there, like a bomb on the verge of exploding.

When she rapped on his door, he jolted. Embarrassing, but at least unwitnessed.

He opened the door, noticing she wore a dress similar to the red dress from Friday night. This one was sunshine-yellow. *How appropriate.*

As she entered, she kissed him and handed over the cat, who butted Devin's chin with his furry head. "Is everything okay?" she asked. "How'd the meeting with Reid go? I've got some ideas about the case you need to hear. What's that glow?" Before he could answer, she'd charged down the hall. "If Howard has some alien experiment—"

She ground to a halt, he assumed, because she'd seen the glow was candlelight. *"Oh,"* she breathed.

He'd do anything—traffic duty, tactical maneuvers, even prison—just to hear that sound on a daily basis. He was falling so hard and fast, it was a wonder the g-forces didn't snap him in half.

"I guess they're not charging you with murder."

The oddness of their conversation wasn't lost on him. "Not yet."

"So we're celebrating?"

Still holding Sharky under one arm, Devin slid the other around Calla. "Definitely."

"This is beautiful." She turned and laid her hands on his shoulders. "Thanks."

Devin absorbed her warmth. "I'll feed the cat. You open the wine."

While Sharky devoured his tuna, they enjoyed their drinks and salads. "What happened today?" she asked.

The last thing Devin wanted to talk about was his problem, but he knew he had to give Calla something. "Reid didn't ask many questions. I don't think his heart was in it."

Calla paused with her fork halfway to her mouth. "He has a heart?"

"Not sure. But he was distracted. Maybe some other cop's in bigger trouble than me." Frankly, he thought Reid was way too easy on him. Something was up, and he'd already tapped his inside contacts to find out what. "So Howard and I went to his office and talked about my old cases. He asked me to leave the files with him, which I did. Fresh eyes would be good."

"Shelby and Victoria want to help."

"And I appreciate that, but they have their own lives, and tonight we have ours."

"We had the weekend together."

He smiled. "Is it any wonder I want more?"

"Me, too, but I did some research, and I have a theory I want to run by you."

He both hated and appreciated that she was so worried about him. "You can't spend every second of your day focusing on me."

"Why not?"

"You can, I guess, but I wish you wouldn't."

"Why?"

"I want to focus on you."

When she opened her mouth—to argue, no doubt—

he pulled her close and kissed her, which fell more in line with his plans for the night than hers. "Tomorrow," he mumbled against her lips. "Big meeting, the whole gang. We'll come up with a plan of attack."

Sighing with pleasure, she rubbed her cheek against his. "I need to tell the gang we're not meeting tonight."

"Already done."

"I also need to tell you what I've come up with. It won't take long, and then I promise to let this go until tomorrow."

He could deny her nothing. Leaning back in his chair, he toasted her with his wineglass. "Go ahead, Detective Hood."

Her lips formed in a happy smirk at the new title. "So, I definitely think a woman is involved, and here's why…"

She proceeded to outline her reasoning for revenge and the steps that had led to both Devin's framing and Jimmie's death. While part of him thought she was bending the facts to suit her theory, the conjecture made sense. For this woman, an unstable accomplice could blow the revenge scheme. "You should contact somebody in Homicide who can give you the autopsy results ASAP. What about the guy you worked with on the East River case last spring?"

"Carl Anderson. Already done."

Her eyes widened. "Really?"

"I hung with him and his case awhile, and he's a sharp guy. He'll see the setup against me. Let's eat."

She glanced down at her nearly empty salad plate. "We are."

He retrieved the insulated container of chicken and pasta, which he dished out to both of them. "I'd hate for Shelby's creation to get cold."

She undoubtably knew he was subverting the tougher questions of homicidal women from his past, but she met his gaze and picked up her fork. "Me, either."

"What's your father like?" he asked as they started on dinner.

"Big, stern—except with me, of course—hard working, independent. Very much a Texan."

"Would he like me?"

"As a cop and a guy, sure." Calla twirled pasta around her fork. "As a male who's touching me, no."

Devin knew he wasn't worthy of her, but he was bothered to hear her say it so plainly. "Why not?"

"Because he still wants me to be five and playing with dolls, not playing with men."

"Ah. What about your mom?"

"*She'd* like you. You want to meet them?"

No was his swift, instinctive response, though he had the sense not to voice it aloud. "You think that's a good idea?"

She paused with her hand around her wineglass. "Probably not. Let's get the assault charges dismissed first."

"That's a good idea. What does he think about you living in the city?"

"He's not crazy about it, but he knows this is where I'm happy."

"Think you'd ever go back home?"

"No. New York is home now. Did you grow up here?"

"Queens. I don't want to go back there, either."

"You must have had some good times."

"School was okay." Regular meals served anyway. "I liked playing sports."

"Which ones?"

"Baseball and football. We probably couldn't have

done much against any teams from Texas, but we didn't suck, either."

"Sports are a religion in Texas," she agreed. "Football especially." Leaning forward, she propped her chin on her fist. "I wouldn't have pegged you for a team sport. What position did you play?"

"Fullback."

"Ah, the muscle. Now, that I can see."

"I had some issues with aggression. Football helped me channel my energy into something positive."

She sipped her wine. "Is that also why you became a cop?"

"Plenty of people around me made the wrong choices. I didn't want to end up like them. I turned eighteen and headed straight for the academy."

"That's a long time to be a cop."

"My life."

"Which will continue."

Watching the candlelight flicker across her flawless skin, he decided his singular purpose in life was over-rated. "I'll get right on that." He stood and held out his hand. "For now, I only want to dance with you."

When she moved into his arms, he closed his eyes and breathed in her warm, floral perfume. Her body brushed his as they swayed to the wail of a saxophone, and he relished the slow build of desire coursing through him.

All day, subjected to questions about his judgement and integrity, he'd dreamed of her touch, her devotion and hunger for him. He'd fought side by side with the law for more than a decade, but nothing had earned him anything as amazing as her.

He wished he could believe in the two of them to-gether.

But with his career and freedom in jeopardy, he had no right to dream beyond getting back what he'd had before—a badge, a gun and a distant longing for something wonderful that always seemed out of reach.

For now, though, he and Calla were a team, and he'd learned the merits of a gang were wildly underrated by the department.

He'd never had an intimate partner. Lovers, sure, but not a true partner. On the force, he'd worked with different guys, but Meyer had quickly discovered Devin liked solitude. Maybe he always would.

"Where'd you go?" Calla asked softly in his ear.

"Sorry." He brushed his lips across her cheek. "You're right. It's hard to set aside my case."

She leaned back slightly, her eyes full of promise. "Let's try—for a little while, anyway."

11

CALLA WOKE TO BOTH purring and pounding in her ears.

She tucked her head between Devin's neck and shoulder. "Sharky's hungry," she mumbled.

His arms slid around her while one hand moved down her bare thigh. "He can wait."

She pressed her lips to his throat. "And my head's throbbing. I don't remember drinking that much wine."

"We didn't." He rolled on top of her, his erection pressing against her hip. "I'm throbbing, too. Wanna help me out?"

While her body involuntarily responded with *Yes, yes, I do!*, Calla flattened her palm against his chest. "Cheesy, Devin. Really. I hear pounding."

He cocked his head. "It's the door. What time is it?"

"No idea." Her gaze was glued to him. Maybe she'd been too hasty. He was so sexy with his sleepy eyes and inky, mussed hair. She pulled him closer. "Whoever it is will come back."

He rolled off her, scooped a revolver off the bedside table and pulled on his jeans. "Stay here," he ordered.

"Guess I'll feed the cat," she muttered as Sharky

butted his head against hers and amped up the purring another notch.

She padded into the bathroom to brush her hair and teeth, then looked around for something to wear.

Hearing two male voices at the end of the hall, she amended her wardrobe of Devin's T-shirt, which only hung to midthigh and added a pair of sweatpants she found in his dresser. She might look sloppy, but she wasn't wearing her dress from last night at seven-thirty in the morning.

As she opened the bedroom door, she saw Lieutenant Reid walking into the living room. Not exactly the way she wanted to start her day.

"I started coffee," Devin said, moving toward her. "Take this," he whispered in her ear, pressing something hard against her stomach.

The gun.

Good grief. She was going to need a nice, long spa weekend when this whole mess was over.

She exchanged the cat for the weapon and tried not to think about the irony of the innocent and the deadly. After tucking the gun into the nightstand drawer and grabbing a T-shirt for Devin, she headed straight for the coffeemaker, where he was watching the final drips flow into the pot.

She handed him the shirt. "What's going on?" she whispered.

"No idea. Reid looks like he got a lot less sleep than we did, though."

Together, they carried the cups into the living room. As they settled on the sofa, Reid remained standing. The precise, well-groomed man who'd shown up at this same apartment only days before had bloodshot eyes, wore a stained and wrinkled tie and was pale enough to see through.

He accepted his coffee and took a sip. "Thanks. It was a long night."

Calla decided if she was going to be accused of being Pollyanna, she might as well fulfill her role. "Are you here to tell us the case against Devin has been dismissed?"

"Unfortunately, no." Reid reached into his briefcase and pulled out a file folder. "An informant saw the news report about Jimmie's death and came to the station last night, claiming he saw Devin buying heroin on Saturday night."

Fury blazed through Calla. *What?* He was with me the entire—"

Reid held up his hand. "I know. After I challenged the informant with Devin's alibi, he became flustered. He changed his story, claiming a woman gave him two thousand dollars in cash to go to the police with the bogus story."

"You believe him?" Devin asked.

Reid nodded. "He still had a wad of hundreds in his pocket."

"What woman?" Calla asked.

"A blonde, though the informant thinks she was wearing a wig. And before you jump all over me, Ms. Tucker, the rest of the description doesn't match you. She's attractive, but shorter and thinner. She doesn't have your obvious femininity."

As Reid pushed the open file across the table, Calla wondered if *obvious femininity* was the lieutenant's restrained way of telling her she had a nice rack.

While Devin and Calla studied the sketches—one of a woman's face partially obscured by sunglasses, the other full-bodied—Reid asked, "Do you recognize her? Could she have been the thief you chased, Detective? Maybe she lured you to the alley, and Jimmie knocked you out."

"It's possible," Devin said, glancing up at Reid. "We've actually been working with the theory that Jimmie posed as the thief and she hit me."

Calla glared at the lieutenant. "Devin mentioned the possibility of an accomplice from the beginning. If you'd *listened* to your fellow cop, instead of arresting him, you could've saved yourself a lot of time."

"I never believed Devin assaulted Jimmie," Reid said calmly. "I don't think he killed him, either."

"So why'd you arrest him?" Calla asked in disbelief.

"The evidence couldn't be ignored," Reid explained.

Since the evidence was a mass of contradictions, that was the dumbest, most shortsighted reason Calla had ever heard. Bureaucratic nonsense. Still, she made an effort to rein in her temper. Anger would only cloud her thoughts. Somebody needed to display a little sense.

But the injustice burned her up. What kind of Sherwood Forest was the NYPD running?

His expression blank, Devin stared at Reid. "Why don't you think I'm guilty?"

"The assault was too candy-ass. Not your style."

"And Jimmie was murdered?"

"The M.E. thinks so," Reid said. "There was no sign of a struggle on his body or in the apartment, but neither were there previous needle marks. Also, he'd consumed a sedative an hour before his death. The pills were found in a prescription bottle with the label peeled off, but no other evidence of illegal drug use."

"And if it was suicide," Devin added, "he didn't need the heroin. He could've swallowed all the pills."

Reid's lips turned up in a tired smile. "Exactly."

Calla wasn't sure about Devin, but she wasn't ready to be pals with Reid. "So why are you telling us all this now?"

"I'd like your help." Reid pulled a thick, accordion-style file from his briefcase. "Based on your stakeout the other night, it's obvious you're conducting your own investigation. We might as well combine our efforts. It's clear somebody's set you up. If we figure out who's behind the scheme, we'll clear your name and find Jimmie's killer."

"So you're dismissing the charges," Devin said.

Reid winced. "Not yet. As far as anybody other than us and a few key people in the department know, you're still on the hook for Jimmie's assault and suspected of his murder."

Calla barely managed to keep her jaw from dropping. "You're kidding."

"We don't know how far the conspiracy reaches," Reid reasoned. "I want the killer to think he—or more likely in this case *she*—is getting away with the frame. I don't want her making any more moves until we have time to investigate."

"Who are the key people?" Devin asked.

"My captain, Lieutenant Meyer and Anderson from Homicide. I think you know him. He's been assigned to investigate Jimmie's murder."

Devin looked unimpressed by Reid's we're-all-on-the-same-team-but-in-secret proposal. "Why should we trust you?"

Reid met Devin's gaze. "I go after dirty cops. I don't ruin good ones." He dropped the file on the coffee table. "That's everything I've got."

Devin slid his hand down Calla's back. "What do you think, babe?"

Babe? Delight flooded Calla, both at the unexpected endearment and the realization that he was asking her advice before committing to Reid. "I'm not sure we can trust him, but we could use his information."

"I agree." Devin shifted his attention to Reid. "You've got a deal."

Reid didn't comment on their doubt. He was probably used to other cops treating him with suspicion.

Digging into the case file, they discovered Devin's fingerprints from only his right hand had been found on the pipe used to assault Jimmie. How likely was it that he hadn't touched the pipe at all with his other hand? Also, the pipe had been found against the brick wall of the alley, fifteen feet from where Jimmie and Devin fell, which explained why Devin hadn't noticed it when he regained consciousness.

So Devin had beat up Jimmie, knocked himself out then tossed the pipe away? *That dog don't hunt,* as her friends in Texas would say.

"You see those notes about the pipe?" Devin asked her.

"Could it have rolled over there?" Calla mused, glancing at Reid.

"Not that far," the lieutenant answered. "You can see why I was skeptical from the beginning."

Like the assault, Jimmie's murder was planned and organized, but ultimately flawed. Was that because the killer was so focused on revenge that she wasn't thinking clearly, or because she simply wasn't intelligent enough to pull off a complicated conspiracy?

"People who think cops are stupid piss me off," Reid added.

Reid's frustration and exhaustion had clearly allowed him to loosen up, and she was actually beginning to like him. "You figure she planned on you buying Jimmie's story and not looking too deeply into the inconsistencies?"

"She certainly doesn't understand cops."

"No respect for them, either," Calla pointed out. "If this woman is framing Devin because he arrested her or someone she cares about, she's getting back at him for doing his duty. Devin's only the instrument of the law."

"Unless it's more personal." Reid looked toward Devin. "I know I asked you yesterday, but you're sure there's not an ex-girlfriend out there who has it in for you?"

Devin looked amused. "Except for the one in prison, no."

Calla's hand clenched around the stack of pictures she held. "She's still there, isn't she?"

"She is." Reid's eyes gleamed as his gaze roved her face. "And it's nice to see the detective's choices have greatly improved."

"Look all you like, Reid," Devin said, his tone dangerously soft. "But don't even think about touching her."

She belonged to Devin, all right. But for how long?

Since that wasn't a subject she wanted to dwell on, she went back to looking through the photos.

The shots of Jimmie's battered face and body were graphic and jarring, and Calla felt a moment of pity for the squirrelly thief. What had his partner promised him to go along with the scheme? Money? Could've been about sex, too. Or simply revenge against the cop who'd arrested and testified against him.

"I see you considered the idea I had a co-conspirator," Devin said, reading from the file.

Reid poured himself more coffee. "I tried to look at the conflicting facts from all angles. If you'd had a partner who'd knocked you out after you'd beat up Jimmie, then he could have tossed the pipe away."

"Then where are his prints?" Devin argued. "And why leave the pipe at the scene?"

"He wouldn't." Reid leaned back in his chair. "Every time I lined up the evidence against you, the results simply didn't make sense. Especially for a cop."

After another hour of studying the information and becoming frustrated that a miraculous smoking gun hadn't appeared, Calla headed to the kitchen for a snack.

At least Reid's notes and supposition had confirmed their own ideas, and, in her mind at least, her theory about the killer considering herself an avenging angel was not only alive but probable.

Yet how were they going to find her? The cops would ask Jimmie's neighbors and show them the sketch. And the crime scene techs had collected hair and fibers from the murder scene. She couldn't possibly have been in Jimmie's apartment and not left DNA somewhere. So if she was in the criminal database, they'd have a great lead. If not, they—

"Oh, no." She nearly dropped the block of cheese she'd pulled out of the fridge. "The scrap of gold fabric."

When she'd shown it to Devin last week, he hadn't given her much hope that it was connected to his case. But that was before the idea of Jimmie's partner being a woman emerged.

Across the room, Devin was asking Reid about the angle of the pipe blows, and maybe it was possible for a crime scene expert to determine the height of Jimmie's attacker.

Her heart pounding with guilt, Calla dug in her purse

for the evidence, which she'd sealed in a plastic zip bag. She had the dreaded feeling the lieutenant wasn't going to be quite as nonchalant as Devin had been.

No fool in the strategy department, she sliced the cheese and some cured sausage, then assembled the snack on a plate with a variety of crackers. The guys mumbled their thanks, and she waited until their mouths were full before broaching the subject of the item she was holding behind her back.

"Hey, Lieutenant," she began. When he looked her way, she managed to swallow her nerves. "It's Colin, right?"

As he nodded, Devin furrowed his brow. Her sweet tone was probably too much.

"I, ah…found this near where Jimmie and Devin were assaulted." She handed him the plastic bag. "I'm sure it's nothing, but maybe the lab should do some tests or something."

"Where?" was Reid's single, terse question.

"On a shrub at the alley entrance." Calla didn't think she would have trusted him with the information before today. "I remember smelling gardenias when I picked it up."

"From the foliage or the fabric?" Reid asked.

A little put out by his smart-aleck question, Calla crossed her arms over her chest. "Gardenias bloom in the spring."

"You think it could be something?" Devin asked Reid, though he'd already made his doubt clear.

Reid laid the bag on top of the file. "Probably not."

"Your guys still missed it," Calla said smartly.

"Unless it was caught there after we left," Reid reminded her. "When did you two go by?"

Calla sighed. "The next day."

Reid shrugged. "I'll have the techs at the lab look at it. You never know."

The guys dug into their snack again, and Calla joined them. Food was comfort and inspiration according to Shelby. And they could use some of both.

When Reid's phone rang, he moved into the kitchen to talk, and Calla moved into Devin's lap. "What should Reid's gang name be?"

He pressed his lips beneath her jaw. "He doesn't get one. He's a reluctant ally."

"What do you make of his backdoor deal?"

"There are rumors Reid's due a promotion. If he clears me, he could get captain's bars."

"Maybe he simply wants to help a fellow cop. Seems to me he's risking quite a bit by coming to you. Wouldn't the prosecutor have a fit if he found out?"

"He would. Which is why we have to keep quiet and find Jimmie's killer ASAP."

"Given all the contradictory evidence, Howard might be able to get your assault charge dismissed now. You still want to throw your lot in with Reid?"

"We need him," Devin reminded her. "It would be nice to do this as a team."

Devin wanted to play nice with others? A few months ago, Calla would've never believed it possible.

"That was Detective Anderson," Reid said, approaching them. "He's at Jimmie's place and wants us to come by, see if you can spot anything we missed. You know him better than either of us."

"Wonder if he has a gold lamé jacket hidden in the back of his closet?" Calla commented as she pushed to her feet.

After she dressed in jeans and sweater, she gave Sharky a cat treat, then tucked him in his basket. On the way out the door, she was both excited and encouraged. Before they were fighting against the system. Now that they were back on the inside, sort of, anyway, she had a whole new respect for the establishment.

Still, they probably ought to bring their inside man into the fold, legend-wise. "Hey, Colin, what do you know about Robin Hood?"

AT JIMMIE'S APARTMENT, Devin introduced Calla to Detective Carl Anderson and hoped she didn't take his rumpled brown hair and disordered clothes as a measure of his capabilities. His eyes were sharp as a blade.

The apartment was one room and spare, with a generic navy blue chair and sofa that were probably rented, a TV rested on a plastic milk crate and a beige lamp on a wobbly end table.

"Not much in the fridge but leftover Chinese food and beer," Anderson began. "We've dusted for prints. Haven't found any but the vic's."

So none of the people they saw Sunday night came to this apartment? Had he actually slept while the suspect went inside? Could the woman that set off a wrong note have had nothing to do with Jimmie, after all? Had it been a wild leap brought on by desperation for some kind of solid lead? "How long's he been here?"

"Three weeks," Anderson said.

"And no visitors?" Devin asked, surprised. Jumpin' Jimmie scored a Manhattan address and hadn't invited anybody over? "Wait. *No* other prints?"

Anderson smiled. "None."

"He's only been here a few weeks. Where are the former tenant's prints? The furniture has to be rented, which equal moving guys' prints."

"There's a bill from the rental company on the kitchen counter," Anderson told him.

Reid glanced around, suspicion clear in his eyes. "Somebody wiped the place."

"Oh, yeah." Clearly annoyed, Anderson gestured to the room at large. "I see why you brought me in, Colin. This whole deal's off. One, it's too neat in here. Where're the empty soda cans and beer bottles? The TV remote is tucked neatly in the end table drawer. Two, how'd Jimmie afford this place? The forestry service ain't hirin', last I heard."

"Excuse me?" Calla broke in. "Forestry?"

"Jimmie's squirrely," Devin explained. "The woman was the only single person we saw. Everybody else was a family or couples."

"She kept her face turned away from the porch light," Calla reminded him. "Do you mind if I look around?"

Anderson shrugged. "A woman's perspective couldn't hurt. I really hate chick killers."

Calla angled her head. "Why is that?"

"They're meaner," Anderson said simply.

"Good to know." Calla turned and headed straight to the door at the far end of the room that had to lead to a bathroom.

Curious, Devin followed her.

"I know Anderson and his people checked here," she said before he could ask. She wrapped her hand in the scarf around her neck before opening the doors beneath the sink. "When you've got one room, where else are you gonna hide stuff?" She glanced back at him. "Did anybody check the oven?"

Strangely amused and aroused by her crafty thinking, Devin knelt beside her. "No idea."

"They should." She searched the small area, knocking on the walls when nothing jumped out at her. "I've been watching too many spy movies." Blowing out a breath, she pushed to standing—and gasped.

"Those are gardenias."

As she reached for the ceramic pot of white flowers, Devin grabbed her hand. "Don't touch."

"Don't you think that's a wild coincidence?" she asked, pointing at the arrangement beside the sink.

"No. With this case, there are no coincidences. Evidence? Maybe." Devin leaned past the door way. "Anderson, come look at this."

"Flowers?" Anderson questioned, clearly skeptic of how they could be significant. "Yeah, we saw them, dusted the pot. No prints there, either."

"What about the flowers themselves?" Calla asked.

"Not gonna get anything clear," Anderson said. "Why bother?"

Again, Calla wrapped her hand in her scarf as she eased one of the blossoms from the vase. "I'd bother, and I'd check the stems."

"This is about that scrap of gold fabric?" Anderson asked. "Reid gave it to me for the lab to look at. Said it had a floral-like scent."

Calla grimaced, no doubt because of the vague description, then extended the blossom. "Gardenias."

Anderson's gaze moved to Devin. "You think there's anything here?"

The chances that the flowers were connected to the case and would lead to a significant development were so low they were in the single digits. But Calla had been steadfastly loyal to him through everything. No way he'd hurt her feelings by doubting her now. "Could be," he said.

"What the hell." Anderson took the blossom with his gloved hand, then scooped the arrangement off the sink. "We ain't got nothin' else."

12

The New York Tattletale

Farewell Toast and Getting Toasted in Style
by Peeps Galloway, Gossipmonger
(And proud of it!)

This is one of those unfortunate days when I have to fall back on a cliché—do you want the good news or the bad news first?

Since I can't leave you with tragedy, here's the scoop on the bad, bad stuff.... Remember the guy who accused the hottest cop in NYC of assault? (Yes, I *know* it was last week! Focus, people!) Well, he's crossed that great Brooklyn Bridge in the sky. No victim, no trial, right? Rather convenient, wouldn't you say? The cops have closed ranks on this one, and so far, nobody's talking. (Don't fret, my lovelies, I shall not be dissuaded!) In the meantime, I'm thinking what all of you must be: murder charges can't be far behind....

Not that mayhem and murder are going to stop this steadfast reporter from checking out the latest martini bar in Midtown tomorrow night. I know, I know, darlings, been there, done that so many times we've lost count. But Swizzle makes an amazing pomegranate martini with extract from the seeds—which is supposed to be healthy or something, but who cares about *that?* You'll look as cool as hip-hop legend Cameo (who's rumored to hang out there on Thursday nights). Plus, Swizzle is *the* place for the latest trend in mixology— cocktail popsicles. Not just cool, frozen!

Keep calm and keep your ears tuned,
—*Peeps*

"If I ever get my hands on that Peeps Galloway, I'm going to teach her the definition of assault—up close and personal."

Tossing the trashy paper aside, Calla accepted the martini Victoria handed her. "Blue?" she asked, staring at the tinted liquid in the glass.

Victoria held up her own glass. Her drink was purple. "Shelby's experimenting for a wedding. The bride wants cocktails to match her bridesmaids' dresses."

"O-kay." Calla took a sip. The concoction was sweet with a hint of something tropical. "Not bad."

Victoria curled her lip. "Mine tastes like grape-flavored cough syrup."

"You're a martini snob."

"And proud of it."

They were gathered at Shelby and Trevor's for a gang meeting. They'd even invited Howard and Lieutenant Reid, though Devin insisted his lawyer was a consultant and Reid a guest speaker. Calla wasn't sure why they were so exclusive all of a sudden, but with his badge still in Meyer's desk drawer, she wasn't going to push him on his reasoning.

Over the past two days of going through case files— again—probing Devin's memory for the tiniest of details and getting not-so-encouraging updates from Detective Anderson, one thing was clear: this homicidal woman had bested them long enough. It was time to take her down—whoever the heck she was.

So they'd decided to compile all the theories, case files and bits of evidence to see if they'd overlooked something or had anything to go on besides a vague sketch and a vase of white flowers.

Trevor answered the door when the bell rang, and since Howard was the only one not present, Calla assumed he'd arrived.

"Sorry I'm late," the lawyer said, rushing down the hall in front of Trevor. "Traffic was horrible as usual. Instead of cabs, a fleet of hovercrafts would be handy in this city."

"Trevor's been threatening to open a dealership." Shelby headed toward the bar. "What can I get you to drink? The custom martinis are a big hit."

Sitting on the sofa between Devin and Victoria, Calla poked her friend before she could argue with Shelby's sales pitch.

"Scotch and soda would be great," Howard said.

"Why don't we move to the dining room table?" Reid suggested. "I've got several—"

"Sorry to interrupt," Howard said, rising, "but I'd like to say something before we start."

Devin apparently knew what this mysterious announcement was, since he shook his head. "Leave it, Howard."

Howard ignored his client's directive. "If you don't

find this mystery woman, they can still prosecute you for the assault charges."

"We don't want to go to the prosecutor yet," Reid said. "As long as the charges are pending, the killer thinks her plan is working."

Howard's smile was weak. "How nice for her. However, I work for Detective Antonio. I want a guarantee he'll be cleared of the charges and his position with the NYPD restored."

Reid's mouth pulled into a thin line. "I can't do that. This is an undercover operation. Secrecy is imperative, or all our jobs will be on the line."

"My heart bleeds, but, amazingly enough, I don't work for you or Lieutenant Meyer, either." Howard reached into his briefcase and pulled out a piece of paper, which he handed to Reid. "I took the liberty of drawing up a statement I'd like you to sign. If you don't, my client's cooperation with this investigation will be terminated."

"Hell" was Reid's succinct comment.

Howard extended his hands as he addressed everyone else. "Before the Lieutenant chokes, I'll explain to the rest of you that in the statement Reid is agreeing that Devin is innocent of all charges and that he invited Devin to assist in the investigation. As long as the real culprit is found and arrested, I'll destroy the document. If not, I'm going to the D.A."

"I'm really starting to like him," Victoria whispered to Calla.

"Let's just hope we don't have to see that talent in front of a jury," Calla returned.

Reid held out his hand. "Do you have a pen? I've got a job to get back to that doesn't involve extortion."

With pen and statement exchanged, Howard lifted his glass in a toast. "Thank you, sir."

Trevor, impeccable in black pants and a dove-gray shirt, rose with a smile. "Why don't I refresh drinks, while you adjourn to the dining room?"

Calla linked hands with Devin as they crossed the room. "Smile. Robin Hood is on the case."

He didn't, of course, but he squeezed her hand.

He'd been quiet the past couple of days. They'd stayed at her place, since her fridge and pantry were better stocked. He liked standing on her balcony as the sun set, and the lights of the city flickered on like billions of fireflies coming to life at the same time. His lovemaking had been focused and intense and afterward she was pretty sure he slept little, since every time she woke during the night, he was rhythmically stroking her back or arm.

Was he slipping away from her, or holding on till the end of the case? Were past betrayals affecting them as a couple? Or were they building a relationship that meant something?

Not only didn't she know, she couldn't find out.

She was firmly on Detective Anderson's page. She hated chick killers—in more ways than the obvious one.

From behind her, someone put their hand on her shoulder. Turning, she looked up into the smiling brown eyes of Jared McKenna. "Quite a crew you've got here," he said.

"Thanks." She worked up a smile. "I know you're busy. I appreciate you carving out some time."

He winked. "The outdoor adventure business is a whole lot more interesting with you three ladies around."

As they gathered around the table, Reid stood at one

end. "So, it's possible Calla was right about the vase of gardenias she found in Jimmie's bathroom."

Like the time she beat that snotty Virginia Porter in the Miss Sugar and Spice pageant, or the time she won Features Writer of the Year over backstabbing Will Carrier, Calla summoned a gracious attitude and managed not to tell Reid *I told you so.* "Way to lead with a headline, Lieutenant."

As if he sensed the triumph blossoming inside her, he directed his attention to her. "The lab found partial and smudged prints on the flowers as well as the ceramic vase. They're only partials," he repeated. "But there's enough of one print to be certain they aren't Jimmie's. Before everybody gets too excited, we also haven't found a match in the database. For all we know, the print could be from the employee who put together the arrangement at a retail store or manufacturer, some regular Joe who's never been fingerprinted."

"Or it could be from Jimmie's killer," Devin said.

Calla could tell Reid considered that a wild leap. "We're running down where the arrangement came from to see if it's sold separately or already put together," he said neutrally. "But the print itself is likely a dead end."

"Unless you arrest someone to match it to," Calla added.

"Right. Unfortunately, that gets us nowhere in finding a suspect to arrest." The strain of the investigation was etched into Reid's face. "NYPD has used our sketch provided by the informant to canvass Jimmie's apartment building, but, so far, nobody's made a match."

"The informant was bribed to implicate Devin in a drug buy," Trevor pointed out. "How reliable could he possibly be?"

"That's the other problem," Reid admitted. "We think this guy's more scared of us than whoever paid him off, but, ultimately, we have no idea how accurate the sketch is. He could be purposely misleading us."

Victoria drummed her fingernails against the table. "For somebody who's done so many terrible things and made so many apparent mistakes, this woman certainly knows how to get her way."

"We do have one other lead." This time Reid appeared to deliberately avoid Calla's gaze. "The gold fabric Calla found near the alley where the assault took place was torn from a designer handbag."

He *had* buried the lead, Calla realized on a gasp.

Shelby looked confused. "She brought a handbag to commit assault?"

"Maybe she was trying to blend in," Trevor said. "A black ski mask is certainly too obvious. She apparently got away from the scene without anybody spotting her."

"We don't know this is related to our case," Reid said, aggravation causing his face to redden. "Do you know how many of those bags were sold in the last six months in Manhattan alone?"

"Doesn't matter," Calla said. They were on to something. They had to be. "In my book, gardenia-scented fabric plus gardenia arrangement in dead man's bathroom equals killer."

"This isn't solid evidence," Reid argued.

Calla understood cops were restrained by laws, codes and rules the general public weren't—Reid maybe a little more so than others—but they also trusted their instincts. And these minor details that may or may not be solid evidence led somewhere.

If she was right, and this case was about revenge, the symbolism would be important. Gardenias meant something to her, or someone she cared about. Calla would bet her life on it.

Seeing her wavy, mysterious figure in her mind's eye, she couldn't wait to flip vengeance back at the homicidal witch.

Devin shoved back his chair and rose. "So, we have a handbag, an arrangement of gardenias and a sketch given by an unreliable informant who tried to convince the cops he just happened to be standing around when I bought heroin." His gaze swept everyone at the table. "Are you guys sure this isn't some elaborate practical joke?"

Calla, along with the rest of the gang, stared uncomprehendingly at Devin.

"I know I've given you a hard time about interfering in police business," he continued. "Crazy, I guess, for thinking you should do your jobs, while you let us do ours. I get the power of *all for one and one for all,* but—"

"That's the Three Musketeers," Calla, Victoria and Shelby all said at once.

"Okay," Devin conceded. "Whatever your motto is, but I can't get a handle on this case. Gardenias, gold lamé and heroin? Jumpin' Jimmie assaults and frames me?" He shook his head. "I don't get it."

Actually, the whole business made a sick kind of sense to Calla, so she didn't know whether he was finally cracking under the pressure, or she had a strange sense of logic, but she had no idea what to say to him.

Victoria, sitting on the other side of Devin, wrapped her fingers around his wrist and tugged him back to his seat. "Women are complicated creatures, Detective. Don't worry. You're in capable hands."

"Hear, hear." Howard smiled as he lifted his glass.

"Oscar Wilde, as always, is appropriate. *Women are made to be loved, not understood.*"

As the other men nodded in agreement, Calla tried to decide if the statement was an insult or compliment. Women weren't that complicated, were they? And did loved mean *cherished* or *good-for-sex?*

While both were true, she wondered if the latter was more accurate for her and Devin. Were they using each other? She'd had a crush on him for months, and now that the fantasies about intimacy between them had been fulfilled, did they have anything else to build on?

The extreme circumstances they found themselves connected by couldn't be helping. Was he destined to be a hot lover she'd held for a time—or vice versa— then ultimately had to let go?

Since the idea of letting Devin go made her stomach churn, she forced herself to smile at Howard, who, with an almost worshipful attitude toward women, had only been trying to lighten the mood.

"Save it for the courtroom, Howard," Reid said dryly.

Howard waved the document he'd forced Reid to sign. "What courtroom?"

"Thanks for the reminder, Counselor." Reid braced his hands on the table. "Reluctantly, but at Detective Antonio's urging, I've agreed to share sensitive NYPD case files with you. Apparently, your—" he paused before he went ahead "—*group* has had some success with cracking difficult cases. So I have a task for you.

"Over the last few days, we've narrowed down Devin's most likely closed investigations that could be connected to Jimmie. We've eliminated those who are deceased or still in prison. Go through the files and look for a female suspect, or any female connected to any of the men."

Calla stared at Reid. "You want us to look through files?"

"Again?" Victoria asked in disbelief.

Devin could apparently tell relations with Reid were going south, since he shot to his feet. "Thank you, Lieutenant. Leave the files. I'd like a word in private before you go."

They all gave Reid hearty goodbye and waited in silence for Devin to return. Calla clenched her hands together to keep from pounding her fists on the table.

"Look, Calla," Devin began in a consoling tone. "Reid doesn't know the full capabilities—"

Calla stood. "Who votes we sit on the sidelines and do paperwork?"

Devin, naturally, was the only one who raised his hand.

"It's five to one," Calla said smartly. "You lose."

"I thought we'd at least get to do surveillance or something," Shelby said, her disappointment clear.

"We will," Calla promised. "I have a better idea."

"Of course you do." Devin sighed. "I don't think it's a good idea to defy the lieutenant. I seem to remember you people going around me to bring down that investment scheme and your plan falling apart."

Shelby scowled. "That was my plan."

"And we all got to the same place eventually," Calla reminded Devin.

Trevor cleared his throat. "Not to buck your leadership or determination, Calla, but I am a bit worried about our involvement. This isn't an embezzler or a jewel thief we're after this time, it's a killer."

"I know, and we're not taking unnecessary chances," Calla promised. "Neither are we going to defy Reid. We *are* looking through the files, and we *are* pulling out likely suspects. Then we're going to interview them all."

"How?" Victoria asked, clearly skeptical. "Nobody in this room has a badge. Sorry, Devin."

Calla smiled. "We've got something better—the power of the first amendment. We think our killer is getting revenge against Devin for arresting her, or someone she cares about, right? So, we'll tell all our suspects we're writers, doing a story on wrongly imprisoned convicts."

Devin's eyes widened. "I'm not sending you out in reporter-mode to talk to potential killers."

Calla wanted to inform him *he* didn't *send* her anywhere, but chose to keep the peace. For the greater good, of course. "First of all, I won't be the only one interviewing. We'll need everybody in order to cover all the potentials, so we'll go in pairs. The couples can be together. Well, except you, Devin. Our killer knows who you are. Howard, you can pose as my research assistant, can't you?"

Howard not only nodded, he looked wildly thrilled by the prospect.

"I cook," Shelby said. "How am I going to pull off being a professional writer?"

Calla waved her hand. "It's easy. Take a laptop or notebook and ask nosy questions."

"What if someone checks our credentials?" Jared asked.

Calla had already considered and solved that stumbling block. "I'll make business cards for all of you, and my editor will back up a fake resume."

"Aren't we expanding this conspiracy too much?" Victoria wondered. "The more people we tell, the more likely our mission gets exposed."

"My editor at *City Life* worked for the *Washington Post* in his younger days," Calla explained. "He'd go to jail rather than reveal a source. Which I'll tell him all of you are."

"What if no one will talk to us?" Trevor asked.

"That's the beauty," Calla said proudly. "If I'm right about this woman's motivation for getting back at Devin, she won't be able to help herself from talking about injustice. She might lie about why she feels the way she does, but she'll talk."

"And if you're wrong?" Victoria asked.

Calla had no idea what direction they'd turn, but there was no use in worrying about that unless the time came. "We'll think of something else."

"It's a bold plan," Jared said.

"And we don't have anything else," Shelby added.

Though Calla hadn't gotten the rousing ovation she'd been hoping for, she was confident her idea was the best chance they had. Although, the closer they got to closing the case, the closer she and Devin got to a crossroads in their relationship.

She might be the leader of a mythical gang, but she couldn't live in a fairy tale forever.

As DEVIN LISTENED IN silent amazement to his girlfriend and her friends cook up their undercover operation, which couldn't possibly succeed, he idly wondered if he could get a job in private security. Provided Howard was as good as he claimed and he could get Devin off on the assault charge, it might be time to polish his resume.

The money was supposedly better, but what about a pension and health insurance? He'd be picky about the jobs he took, too. He didn't mind taking a bullet to protect his city, but he wasn't taking one for some starlet with a crazed stalker fan who wanted to prove his love by waving around a loaded pistol.

"We can break rules the NYPD can't," Calla was saying, causing him to wince. "Let's use that to our advantage."

Law and order had served him well for over a decade. He simply didn't have the heart for vigilante justice. "I hate to trample all over your big idea, but—"

"But, let me guess," Victoria cut in. "You're going to, anyway."

Devin ignored the sarcasm, which he'd expected. "Conducting an investigation is all about teamwork."

"Like we don't know that?" Calla asked, irritated. "Our teamwork closed two cases in five months."

He also ignored that. "In addition, every investigation has a leader."

"I'm—"

Devin rushed ahead before Calla could remind him about her gang position. "Our leader is Lieutenant Reid. In order to identify a suspect and build a case against her, we have to follow his directives." Not to mention the idea of Calla sitting across the table from a cold-blooded killer made his own blood freeze. "As long as each member of the team does his or her part, the suspect is arrested and prosecuted. That's how the system works."

"Do they teach you how to make scary speeches at the police academy?" Shelby asked.

Calla planted her hands on her hips. "We're not part of the system. The system has, in fact, failed you to this point. That's the whole point of Robin Hood." She turned her back on Devin and faced the table. "Unlike the NYPD, we can lie about whatever we want. We can lift fingerprints off the glass our suspect uses and have them tested against the partials the lab found. No warrant required."

"No, you can't," Devin said slowly and firmly. "You'll taint the chain of evidence. No judge would let that information be heard in court."

Calla waved her hand in dismissal. "We don't need court. We need a suspect. You guys can figure out how to prosecute her once we find her."

Devin was almost certain the top of his head was going to blow off. "Oh, can we?"

"Calla has a point," Trevor said. "This woman has been a shadow so far. The usual methods aren't getting results."

"It's too dangerous," Devin argued.

Calla glared at him over her shoulder. "We'll meet the suspects in public places," she said through clenched teeth. "No one's going to get hurt."

"Really?" Devin faked surprise. "And that guarantee is based on your many years of experience in being safe and nonimpulsive?"

"Trevor, do something," Shelby pleaded.

Trevor pulled out his wife's chair and urged her to her feet. "I have a firm policy not to get in the middle of another couple's argument. Why don't we go upstairs to the terrace?"

Victoria practically leaped out of her seat, grabbing Jared's hand and poking Howard's shoulder. "Great idea."

"There's a full moon," Howard said, following the others. "I should have brought my telescope."

The moment they were alone, Calla pushed her face within inches of Devin's. "Since when do I need your permission to do anything?"

"Since it's my ass on the line."

"I didn't hear you complain when I hauled your drunk ass home from that dive bar and took care of you."

Actually, he'd told her over and over he didn't want to drag her into his dark and precarious life. She never listened.

"Or when I found the only two pieces of physical evidence that gives us any remote lead on the identity of this woman," she continued, her azure eyes standing out starkly from her flushed face.

"Well, now that you've come up with a hairbrained scheme that involves you confronting a killer, I'm objecting."

She jabbed her finger against his chest. "Look here, buddy. I know I said the possessiveness was sexy, but I control where I go and what I do. I'm not some kind of chattel for you to order around."

"Chattel?"

"From Medieval times. It means a personal possession. I was the leader of this group long before Lieutenant Rulebook arrived, and my plan deserves more consideration than your knee-jerk rejection because we're not following the chain of command. Furthermore, any time you and your NYPD pals want to run your little operation by yourselves, be my guest." She stormed off. "Tell Shelby I went home. And you can find some other comfy bed to warm tonight," she added as she stalked down the hall.

"I'm worried about you!" he shouted after her.

She halted at the door. "Why?" she asked without turning around.

Encouraged by her soft tone, he approached her, though he was cautious enough not to touch. "I can't be responsible for you getting hurt."

Her gaze met his, searching. "Why?"

"You mean too much to me."

"I want to help you for the same reason."

But she couldn't possibly realize how thoroughly her beauty and optimism had saved him. Not that he could tell her. Not only wasn't he the schmaltzy hearts and flowers type, he'd never forgive himself for contaminating her rosy light with revenge and death.

She should be writing about exotic beaches and the latest luxury ski resort, not getting her editor to lie so they could interview potential murderers.

He chanced soothing her fury and slid his arm around her waist. "I couldn't do any of this without you. Your plan is good, but risking you is not how I want to get my badge back."

"So help me. We can do this together." She curled her arms around his neck. "You know, teamwork."

He pulled her against him. "We're a pretty good team."

She bumped her hip against his growing erection. "In certain areas, we're great."

They were compatible in bed and nowhere else? Expected, but he had the strange urge to argue. Shouldn't there be more? Did he want more?

He did, but wasn't sure how to say so, much less make it happen. "I want to tell Reid and Anderson," he said, realizing he needed to focus on work, where he actually knew what to do.

"They won't approve."

"They will. They don't have anything else, either." He saw the argument rise in her eyes. "We need backup."

"Okay, fine." After a brief sulk, she kissed him beneath his chin, and his blood, so cool from fear, warmed again. "But if they're around, we'll have to follow rules," she said.

Always the vigilante. "Some, yes, but it's not illegal for law enforcement to mislead a suspect."

She brightened. "So, we can lie. What about the prints?"

"Based on a suspicious statement from a suspect, we might have probable cause for print analysis."

"Who determines what's suspicious?"

"I do."

She scowled. "Don't forget I'm Robin."

He returned her caress, pressing his lips to her chin, then her jaw. A touch he longed to extend and determined he would by night's end. "So you've told me many, many times."

"And from now on, no dismissing my ideas without telling me the real reason you're objecting."

No way he'd share that much. He didn't know how. "I'll be a team player," he said, since that was within his capabilities.

The rest of a healthy relationship was a complete mystery.

13

"HOW DO I LET MYSELF get talked into these things?"
Devin wondered, though no one else was in the surveillance van to hear him complain.

From the case files, the gang had identified the best
leads and each pair of *writers* was interviewing two
suspects a day, mostly during their lunch hour, as everybody had their own jobs to do or businesses to run.

As predicted, several of the women contacted didn't
want to talk, since not only didn't they think their
spouse-boyfriend-brother-uncle had been wrongly convicted, but were thrilled he had been. Those contacts
were added to the backburner.

Yesterday hadn't yielded any dramatic results, but
Calla's confidence wasn't shaken. She'd personally in-
terviewed the two most likely female ex-cons Devin
had arrested who might be revenge-minded. Both were
only too happy to yammer on about how they'd been
railroaded. But since the department had profiled their
murder suspect as cold and remote, the two were eliminated easily. Also, their prints were on file and hadn't
matched any aspect of the partials.

His one stipulation to the fake journalist plan—

putting Anderson and Reid in charge of surveillance—
had eased his mind enough to let the Shelby-Trevor and
Victoria-Jared teams move forward with basic micro-
phones to record what they said to suspects and com-
municate with his colleagues, who were monitoring
from a few blocks away.

But since Calla had drawn the minuscule straw with
Howard, and Devin was extra paranoid when it came
to her, he was taking further precautions. So he'd made
her wear a wire with video capabilities, which he was
monitoring from a utility van across the street from the
café where she was meeting her suspects.

"What an adorable picture," Calla was saying, holding a photograph of their suspect's brother at five.

"You wouldn't recognize him now," Natalie Thompson sobbed. "Shaved head, tattoos, piercings. Prison
changed him. It's horrible."

Exasperated, Devin slumped in his seat. Yeah, poor
little Stevie Thompson. Course today, he was 6'4",
weighed 240 and had a fondness for using a knife with
a ten-inch serrated blade to threaten convenience store
clerks as he robbed them.

Devin had nearly been filleted when he'd arrested
him and was thrilled to know he was still behind bars
where he belonged.

Howard handed Natalie a tissue. "Tragic."

"Thanks." Trembling, Natalie dabbed her eyes. "He
fell in with the wrong crowd, you know. He said the
police planted that big knife on him."

Calla gasped. "You're kidding. That's not fair."

"I know, right?" Natalie blew her nose. "Then they
wouldn't let him out on bail because he'd supposedly
tried to attack the cop who arrested him." Natalie was
busying mopping more tears off her face and didn't no-

tice the shocked expression that crossed Calla's. "Stevie said he hadn't realized the guy was a cop. He'd only been defending himself."

"Yeah," Devin muttered. "The big, shiny badge I shoved in his face wasn't a definitive clue."

"Stevie wouldn't hurt a fly," Natalie wailed.

"But he's awfully…big," Howard commented.

Calla jabbed Howard with her elbow and put on an earnest expression for her suspect. "Of course he wouldn't. Do you think the police are abusing their authority?"

Natalie sniffled as she lifted her watery gaze to Calla's. "I did for a while. I was so prepared to hate the cop that arrested him. I couldn't wait to go to the trial. So, there he was, sitting in the witness stand and looking fierce and remote, but he was also…" She trailed off, apparently lost in a memory.

"But he was also?" Calla prompted.

Natalie's bloodshot eyes lit up. *"Gorgeous."*

Devin nearly fell out of his chair. "You've *got* to be kidding."

Howard looked disgusted, and Calla coughed, likely covering up a laugh.

"I mean I'm loyal to my brother and all," Natalie continued. "I wasn't going to ask him out or anything like that. But if the NYPD's got guys like that roaming the city, I'm all for law and order."

"Are you sure you're not more resentful?" Howard asked pleadingly. "After all, good looks are genetic. It's not like he's responsible for them. I think intelligence is a much more reliable yardstick of—"

"He could be dumb as a rock for all I care." Natalie pulled a compact from her purse and dabbed her flushed cheeks. "Anyway, I still don't think Stevie did anything wrong, but I blame his attorney, not the cops. How that idiot got through law school, I'll never know. Course all lawyers are creeps, so what do ya expect?"

Howard suddenly became thoroughly engrossed in taking notes on the pad he'd laid on the table.

"That's where you should put the focus for your article," Natalie said to Calla. "No telling how many innocent people are in prison thanks to incompetent lawyers."

Calla cleared her throat. "I'll certainly give that consideration."

They parted from their suspect with effusive thanks and a promise to send a copy of the article when it was released.

Howard pulled out Calla's chair, and she returned to her seat. Their next interview wasn't for another half an hour, so they ordered lunch.

As the waitress walked away, Calla commented in a low voice, "So, Detective G, think that's our killer?"

Devin moved his headset microphone in front of his mouth. "Detect—" He stopped, realizing the significance. Gorgeous. Isn't that terrific? Maybe he'd be extra popular in prison. "I think we can safely eliminate Natalie Thompson."

"Whatever happened to brains over beauty?" Howard wondered.

Calla squeezed lemon into her water glass. "Don't kid yourself, Howard. Women can be just as shallow as men."

Howard sighed. "You said it, sister."

"Devin, you've got your care package, don't you?" Calla asked.

"Yeah." Though he knew the Robin Hood gang would provide something more interesting than the ham sandwich he usually wound up with during surveillance, he realized he'd be eating while watching his girlfriend enjoy lunch with another man.

Calla laughed at a joke Howard made about the guy at the table next to them, who was apparently having lunch with a lover, but not his wife.

"Maybe you should slip him your business card," Calla suggested quietly.

"I don't do divorces," Howard said, toasting her with his soda glass. "I prefer love and devotion in a relationship."

Devin hunched his shoulders.

Calla was devoted to him, but did he give her what she needed? He was certain he satisfied her, and she loved helping him. Her positive spirit certainly left her open to love, but he wasn't sure he knew how. He couldn't imagine the "L" word was truly part of their relationship. Nor did he necessarily want it to be.

Truthfully, the entire idea scared the crap out of him.

Instead, to show his appreciation for her affection, care and patience, he'd given her a traumatized cat.

"Way to go, Antonio," he mumbled.

"What was that, Devin?" Calla asked. "Is something wrong?"

He'd forgotten about the microphone. "No. Everything's good here."

Even as he said the words, the waitress delivered their meals, and Devin ground his teeth as Howard offered to grind pepper over Calla's salad.

Wasn't suppressed anger bad for digestion?

At least when he opened his picnic basket, he found a bowl containing several varieties of lettuce leaves with all the salad additions and dressing packed in individual plastic containers, one of which included medium rare, thinly sliced prime filet.

There was a note from Shelby. *If you're going to live on beef, you should at least have some greens.*

Care and devotion. Yet he hadn't even satisfied Shelby beyond arresting the guy who'd stolen her parents' retirement savings.

Oscar Wilde was obviously right on point.

After surviving lunch—barely—and reminding his chummy investigative duo that the suspect was five minutes away, Devin double-checked all the audio and video equipment. He briefly, and silently, acknowledged that Howard was way better at romance than he could ever dream to be.

Devin wasn't blind. He knew he was bigger, stronger and more physical than Howard, but his lawyer knew the right things to say, how to engage a woman in a conversation she enjoyed, how to make her laugh and relax, how to show her she was valued beyond the bedroom.

Devin was clueless.

With little choice, he shook off his inadequacies and doubts as the second interview began. The information revealed was as unlikely to lead to anything significant as the discussions before it.

The suspect seemed more interested in her free lunch than chatting about her ex-boyfriend, who was doing time for aggravated assault.

She blamed his mother, her mother, the government, the cops and his hard-drinking buddies for his problems. Yet she seemed too angry. She had no control and certainly didn't have the sophistication to pull off the elaborate frame-up their suspect had. And, at 5'9", 200 pounds and sporting both a scorpion tattoo and blue-streaked hair, she looked nothing like the sketch.

Scary, but not their killer.

"We've got nothing," he said to Calla and Howard as Blue-haired Girl left. "Let's meet Anderson and Reid to see if they've got anything better."

SINCE THEY WEREN'T officially part of the gang, Devin's colleagues hadn't gotten a care package, so they suggested a meeting and late lunch at a sports bar near Times Square.

They might be surrounded by too much neon and chatty tourists, but they couldn't chance Paddy's, the usual cop hangout. They'd have to explain why a suspended detective was sharing a cozy meal with IAB and the Homicide cop in charge of the case of the guy he'd been accused of assaulting.

Personally, Devin was already sick of the intrigue. He'd never make it as a long-term undercover guy.

The gang, including Howard, had to go back to their respective offices, so that left Devin, Calla, Anderson and Reid.

Anderson flipped open his menu. "So…Detective Gorgeous, the captain's been tryin' to get a Men of the NYPD calendar started up. You play your cards right, you could be Mr. October."

Humiliated, Devin closed his eyes. "How did you—"

"It's my op," Anderson said, his tone matter-of-fact. "I can listen to whatever channel I want to."

He was absolutely never going to live that one down. Would he also be called a coward if he took a job in private security and never had to walk through the doors of the station again?

Calla shrugged. "Beauty aside, Detective, which is entirely subjective, the more embarrassing fact is that it's a bad boy thing. Some women simply can't resist the lure."

No kidding?

Wait, based on her hand currently sliding across his thigh, she was kidding.

Still, Devin considered her comment. The *bad boy* moniker seemed more apt for movie trailers or extreme sports. But was that description why she was interested in him? Had she been lured? Was he a curiosity? A distraction?

He found himself unhappy by all those reasonings. But what else did he have to offer her?

"This is a murder investigation." Reid snapped closed his menu and laid it on the table. "Can we focus?"

"Just tryin' to lighten the mood," Anderson retorted, unrepentant. "I'll have the cheeseburger," he added to the waitress.

Reid ordered a club sandwich, and they were left to talk about their unproductive morning.

Reid claimed their second interview was a possibility. The suspect was infuriated over her son's arrest and conviction for drug possession and intent to sell, and she wasn't going to take it anymore. She was certain Devin had planted evidence—apparently a common delusion among the wrongly convicted—and the cops wanted her son in jail because he knew the attorney general was a secret communist trying to gain control of the city.

Again, in Devin's option, she harbored too much anger, and she didn't remotely fit the parameters of the sketch.

Were they putting too much emphasis on the stone-cold profile provided by the department shrinks? Since they were usually right, Devin chose to believe they simply hadn't found the right suspect.

What about the sketch? Maybe the informant had deliberately misled them.

In the past few days, Devin had had an opportunity to review the videotaped interview and decided, like his colleagues, the informant didn't have the nerve to deceive the police. He actually reminded Devin of Jimmie.

So their killer picked weak accomplices with shaky reliability. Was that because she was confident in her own talent at avoiding the law, or because she knew she'd eventually eliminate any connection to her?

NYPD had the informant in protective custody, so she wasn't getting to him anytime soon. Did that frustrate her? Or was it part of her plan?

"We've eliminated several people," Calla said, always the optimist.

"And quickly," Reid added.

Anderson took a long swig of his soda. "So we keep at it."

"We're bound to hit on something useful," Reid said.

Devin scowled. "Let's hope we get something besides everybody in this city thinking we're all corrupt and out to get them."

"Hear, hear," Anderson agreed.

Over lunch they talked about the assignments for the following day. Each team had two more interviews to conduct, and if those didn't yield any results, they'd have to dig through the less likely files.

They were waiting for the waitress to bring their check when Reid's phone rang. The conversation was brief, but Reid's voice changed from tired professional to excited cop almost immediately.

Calla tapped Devin's leg to get his attention, and he shrugged, having no idea whether Reid's enthusiasm was a good or a bad thing for him. Oddly enough, his thoughts turned to the statement Howard had forced Reid to sign. Though Devin wasn't big on trust, he understood blackmail.

Reid wouldn't betray him at this stage of the game.

After flagging down their waitress, Reid signed off and dropped his phone in his jacket pocket. "Let's go. We've got a witness who thinks she saw our suspect."

CALLA AND DEVIN WERE shuttled behind the two-way window of interrogation room one, while Reid and Anderson questioned the witness.

"I still don't understand why we can't be part of the interview," she said, annoyed.

"I'm not supposed to be working on this case." Devin guided her to the metal folding chair beside him. "Relax. We're finally getting a break."

After all the wrong turns, fruitless searches and unconfirmed theories, were they actually on the verge of identifying the killer?

Calla sat.

"I'm sorry for the austerity, ma'am," Reid said, leading a dark-haired woman into the interrogation room. "We need to record and videotape your interview for the record."

The woman was a surprise. She was very attractive and fashionable. Her dark brown hair was expertly highlighted, she wore a trendy black-and-white outfit with a rust-colored scarf flung around her neck, and Calla could swear she'd seen her designer wedged heels in a magazine with an accompanying six-hundred-dollar price tag.

Clearly nervous, the witness's gaze flicked to the two-way window. "Please state your name and occupation for the record," Reid said.

"Monica Galloway. I'm a journalist."

Calla gasped. "I absolutely don't believe it. That's Peeps Galloway."

"Who?" Devin asked.

"That crazy chick who writes gossip articles for *The Tattler*. Journalist, my ass."

"You're a reporter?" Anderson asked in surprise.

Nerves apparently overcome, Monica aka Peeps smiled widely. "The best, sweetie."

Reid and Anderson exchanged a skeptical glance.

"We need to get a message to them," Calla said frantically to Devin as she paced in front of the window. "That woman doesn't have information, she's trying to get a scoop."

"She'll be disappointed," Devin assured her. "Reid and Anderson are pros. They won't tell her anything they don't have to."

Like that would stop the woman. Recalling all the details Peeps had gotten on the Robin Hood adventures over the past few months, Calla's heart threatened to jump out of her chest. If she somehow hurt Devin's case to serve her trashy, unethical, ridiculous column…well, she'd be hiring Howard for her own trial. "But—"

"And if she prints anything after the interview that compromises an open case, she'll find herself on the wrong side of jailhouse bars."

"Does she *know* she can't publish anything?" Calla asked.

"No idea." Devin's eyes sparkled. "I imagine Reid will make that clear before he lets her go but after he gets all the information he needs."

"What publication do you work for?" Anderson asked Peeps, his tone less comforting than Reid's.

"I have a column in *The Tattler*."

The disappointed expression on Reid's face was almost comical. "You're Peeps? The gossipmonger?"

Peeps winked. "And proud of it, darling."

Like Calla, Anderson and Reid no doubt now considered this once-promising interview as a giant waste of time. "You have information for us?" Reid asked, sitting across from Peeps, while Anderson wandered around the room.

Calla turned to Devin. "Please tell me they're going to do good cop/bad cop and that Anderson can be really, really mean when he plays his role."

"Anderson interrogates way more scary people than a gossip columnist. If he needs to, he'll have her trembling so badly, she won't type a coherent word for a month."

Satisfied, Calla faced the window, eager to see the show.

"Last night," Peeps began, leaning forward in apparent excitement, "I went out to Swizzle and—"

"What's Swizzle?" Anderson asked.

Peeps stared at him in astonishment. "You're kidding, right?"

Anderson simply crossed his arms over his chest.

"I really need to sponsor a Cop's Night Out," Peeps mumbled. "It's a bar. They specialize in exotic martinis. I had a—"

Anderson glanced at his watch. "It's three o'clock on Friday. You're just now coming to us. Why?"

"I went to Swizzle last night," Peeps said, more slowly this time, as if she were unsure of Anderson's level of intelligence.

"Let her finish," Reid commanded, pretending irritation at his colleague.

"They're throwing her off her pace," Calla realized.

"If her story is rehearsed, she'll have a hard time recovering and making her account sound plausible."

"It works" was Devin's comment.

"So, anyway…" Peeps began, her tone brisker. "I was at Swizzle. It is *the* hot spot for October, so the place was packed as usual, though Cameo didn't show up as rumored."

Anderson and Reid were either fascinated or hip hop music fans, since neither asked who Cameo was.

"Naturally, I had a pomegranate martini," Peeps continued. "They extract nutrients from the actual seeds, so you can apparently get trashed and still feel healthy. Since I was in work-mode, I, naturally, had only one." Her gaze swung to Reid's. "People do all sorts of scandalous and wonderful things when they're tipsy. I once sent a case of Hypnotic to a pop star's hotel room and was first on the scene when she appeared at a CD signing naked. So, anyway, this blond chick strides up to the bar. She was striking even though that hair was very last summer. Oh, and there had to be extensions because there was simply too much volume for *au naturel*. The bartender snapped to attention immediately, and she ordered a bottle of champagne." Peeps frowned. "I mean people drink champagne cocktails in the summer and over the holidays. Otherwise, they're strictly passé."

Calla didn't have to turn to imagine Devin's eyes glazing over the same way Anderson's and Reid's were.

Calla, however, was at full attention. In between the frivolous notes were vivid details. If she'd concocted this story, she was a much better writer than Calla had given her credit for.

Peeps tapped her dark green painted fingernail against the table. "That iron-stomached chick drank every drop of champagne herself in less than two hours, then started on a second bottle. She didn't eat anything, and she expertly deflected all attempts to be picked up—by men, women and anybody in between. Well, since Cameo was MIA and there were no exhibitionist pop stars around, I gradually moved closer until I was sitting on the bar stool next to her. She toasted me and said she was celebrating. She was secretive about why at first, but I ask questions for a living, so it wasn't too difficult to get her to spill, considering her seriously altered state."

Calla could tell Reid was losing his patience with all the unnecessary details and the general silliness. "And this is connected to Detective Antonio's assault case how, exactly?"

"She mentioned him by name," Peeps said, as if this were obvious. "She said he'd finally gotten what he deserved, and she couldn't wait to see him led off in chains."

Devin must have realized the cautious excitement building in Calla, since he commented, "Quite a co-incidence."

Naturally, he was right. How did they know this incident had even happened? Peeps could be making it all up. In fact, she had to be.

Thankfully, Reid also wasn't so easily swayed, though he kept his delivery calm and even. "Antonio has arrested a number of people during his career. Maybe even this woman you saw. She probably heard about the case in the media and is simply happy he's unable to do his job."

As if genuinely mulling over the idea, Peeps cocked her head. "I don't think so. She's got these scary, hard eyes—even when she's toasted. I think she's directly involved in this case. I always thought it was strange

Detective Antonio had been accused in the first place. I've covered him extensively, you know," she added in a low, confident voice. "What if he's been framed, and this woman is responsible?"

"Well, I'll be damned," Calla muttered. She and Peeps were on the same page.

"Anything else?" Reid asked neutrally.

Peeps pursed her brightly painted pink lips as she considered. "She rambled on about chess a few times. Something about the best use of pawns. But I don't play the game. Seriously? Who does?"

Pawns like Jimmie?

Calla's excitement shifted from a distant tingle to an outright buzz. Crazy Peeps Galloway had dropped their best lead right into their laps.

"You didn't document the conversation?" Reid asked, leaning back in his chair as if he couldn't care less, though he most certainly did. "Reporters often carry recorders."

"I don't. At least not last night." Peeps looked disappointed by her mistake. "I was carrying an original Samoian cocktail bag. I could barely squeeze a lipstick in there, and my assistant had my phone. She was waiting to video—hopefully—Kerry Castle cheating on her new husband with her old flame, Drake Mastrano. Hey, do you guys have a video and microphone that could be contained in a lip gloss container? I've appealed to the FBI, but they're reluctant to share."

"Did you identify yourself?" Anderson asked, aggressively bracing his hand on the table beside her. "Maybe she recognized you and was attempting to get her name in the paper."

Peeps glared up at him. "She didn't know who I was. The secret to getting people to tell me everything is to, you know, be secretive. Very few people know what I look like." She paused. "And I'd like to keep it that way. You guys aren't going to blab my identity all over the city, are you?"

"Blab her..." Calla started, then shook her head, wondering if she'd actually heard the wildly arrogant and ironic question Peeps had asked or if the stress of the investigation was affecting her senses.

While she tried to gather herself, Anderson and Reid argued with Peeps over her statement for another couple of minutes, questioning her conclusions and observations, trying to find inconsistencies.

Peeps never wavered.

Much as Calla doubted in the beginning, she was fully on board by the end.

Devin had said little during the interview, and though she was still trying to work out her own hope and worry, Calla sat beside him and grasped his hand. It was his freedom, future and career they were fighting for, after all. "Peeps knows the killer."

Since she'd expected him to argue over her bold conclusion, she was surprised when he squeezed her hand. "Too bad she doesn't have a picture, name or address stowed in her tiny cocktail bag."

Calla had gotten so excited by the break in the case, she hadn't jumped forward far enough to realize that while their theory had been basically confirmed, they were actually no closer to getting their hands on the suspect than before.

"We'd like you to look at a sketch," Reid said, easily avoiding any guarantee about exposing Peeps's identity. He slid a piece of paper across the table toward his witness. "Does this look like the woman you saw last night?"

Peeps slapped her hand on the paper without so much as a glance at its wording. "I don't want my name and image released to the media. I can't do my job if every potential scandal-maker in the city knows what I look like."

Reid, obviously giving up on his good-cop persona, narrowed his eyes. "I can't do my job unless you cooperate fully with an investigation that could ruin a good cop's life and career. Look at the sketch, Ms. Galloway."

Leaning back in her chair, Peeps shook her head. Calla winced, reminded of her own stubbornness, though she admired the other woman's instinct for self-protection.

"When did everybody become so damn distrusting?" Reid wondered in obvious frustration.

Anderson dragged over another chair and sat next to Reid. "We guarantee not to reveal your identity to anyone outside the investigative team."

"Thanks." Peeps glanced at the sketch. "Usually cops don't warrant a mention in my column." She smiled, though her lips trembled. "No offense. I didn't like exposing Detective Antonio's troubles, but he's been featured in the past as a hero, so I did my job and reported the bad with the good. It happens that way sometimes. But if the woman I talked to is trying to hurt him or the NYPD, I'm on board. If I ever have to call 9-1-1, I'd rather not be hung up on."

"The system doesn't work like that," Reid said gently.

"Maybe it should." Blinking back tears, Peeps cleared her throat and picked up the sketch. "This could be her. Hard to tell with the glasses covering her eyes. The hair's almost big enough. Is the sketch artist and/or witness male and fellow cops, by any chance?"

Reid recovered quickly from the off-topic question. "Both are male. One's a cop."

"Well, that accounts for the fact that this woman looks more like something you'd see on a post office bulletin board rather than a gallery on Sixth." Peeps ran her finger over the drawing. "The jawline is right, the narrow cheekbones, the body. With more hair and laser-beam eyes, yeah, this could be her."

"It was reported she wore a wig," Reid prompted.

Peeps shook her head. "Not last night. She was strictly an extension girl." When Reid looked doubtful, she added, "She spends a great deal of time on her appearance, Lieutenant. She wouldn't wear a wig. I've worked with several cancer organizations to provide pieces to cope with hair loss. Thank goodness, there've been many advances. But a trained eye can still tell the difference." She slid the sketch across the table toward him. "I'm a trained eye."

Reid stared at Anderson, who rose. He walked around the table, slowly, never saying a word.

Calla, though on the other side of the glass from him, and knew he was digging into his bad-cop role, shivered.

Finally, Anderson stopped next to Peeps. He bent forward and spoke directly in her ear. "If you're shoving crap in our face, Ms. Galloway, I'll see to it that the next story you write is an extensive exposé on how neither prison orange accessorized by chains and cuffs, nor fake beef stew and instant mashed potatoes are sexy enough to be included in fashion week."

Yep, he was pretty scary.

"I understand," Peeps said in a stronger voice than Calla would have given her credit for.

"So, this suspect…" Reid began, picking up the ball.

"Was she carrying a handbag with gold fabric on it anywhere?"

Peeps seemed surprised, then confident. "No. She—" Another pause. "She didn't have a bag. She paid with cash out of her blazer pocket. Mind you, it was a Pilo Carruba blazer, so the pockets aren't all that large, but I—"

"We'd like you to sit with a sketch artist," Reid interrupted.

Briefly, Peeps's eyes widened like saucers. "Really?"

"Yes." Reid rose. "I think your information is vital to solving our case."

Peeps flipped her long, brown locks over her shoulder. "Certainly, it is. Didn't I say that from the beginning?"

"Anything else at all you can remember about her?" Anderson asked, joining Reid. "A name? Some indication of her profession, where she lived?"

"No, but I did notice she smelled like gardenias."

14

"GOOD HEAVENS, I MIGHT actually have to be grateful to that loony gossip."

Gathering around the table at Shelby's catering kitchen, the most central location for the gang, Devin experienced the oddest combination of comfort, relief and fear at Calla's declaration.

Comfort because the gang had, yet again, rushed to his side as nobody in memory had done. Relief because his nightmare frame-up might actually come to an end, and fear because when it was all over he'd likely lose Calla.

He shouldn't ask her to hang around. He couldn't.

As Calla stalked around Shelby's kitchen, and her friends inexplicably remained silent, Devin knew he had to say something. "She saw the suspect," he said, keeping his voice neutral. "She's our best lead."

"I'm trolling nightclubs with her tonight!" Calla ranted. "That's my assignment for the NYPD."

"You said you didn't want to sit around doing paperwork," Victoria reminded her.

Never had Devin been so grateful for one of Victoria's snarky comments.

Calla stopped moving and shifted her glare to her friend. "How quickly they forget. Do you not recall Labor Day weekend?"

Sitting next to Victoria, Jared grinned.

Would he and Calla ever share another easygoing weekend? Devin wondered. When he had his badge back would their relationship return to the way it'd been before—where he lusted after her from a safe distance, and she went out with other guys while waiting for him to have the guts to do something about their attraction? Or would it simply be over?

He recalled Victoria and Jared's weekend having hit a few bumps, as well. Namely a jewel theft. Somehow they'd worked things out.

"She spied on you and Jared," Calla said sharply.

Victoria looked unconcerned. "She didn't say anything that wasn't true." She laid her hand against Jared's chest. "I remember her being quite accurate where Jared's hotness was concerned."

Shelby brought over a plate of freshly baked cookies, and each of the men couldn't wait to grab one. Devin wondered if the other guys were thinking the same thing he was: with their mouths full nobody would ask them to comment, which would prevent them from getting in trouble with the girls.

Shelby sat next to her husband. "I think we all agree Peeps has been a somewhat…invasive presence in our lives over the last several months."

"My father certainly wasn't pleased to find his name in a gossip rag," Trevor said.

Though that hadn't turned out so bad, Devin recalled. Trevor's father, the Earl of Banfield, had actually joined the gang at one point.

Was there long-term room in the group for a moody,

distrustful cop with a nasty genealogy who was proficient on the firing range, not romancing an alluring woman?

"But this is Devin's career and reputation we're trying to save," Shelby continued, her gaze meeting Calla's. "Whatever we have to do in order to make that happen is a necessary crisis."

Calla nodded. "You're right." Moving behind Devin, she leaned down and wrapped her arms around his neck. "I'm sorry," she said quietly in his ear.

As always, her sweet scent made his head swim. He'd never understand her loyalty. Sure, he'd helped out her and her friends a few times, but he'd only been doing his job. "Have a cookie," he said, handing her one.

Since he got a kiss on the cheek for that, he wondered if this boyfriend business could be learned and made a mental note to ask Trevor and Jared at the first opportunity.

"I want to update all of you, not rant," Calla said after eating her cookie. "With our suspect interviews suspended for now, the cops have come up with a pretty good plan," she admitted. "Even if it does involve that big-mouthed Peeps."

"We have to make deals with lesser cons all the time in order to get the dangerous ones," Devin told her.

"The wheels of justice," Calla commented with a weary shake of her head. "No wonder Robin Hood is always in such high demand." She took another cookie. "So Anderson and Reid think our killer needs attention, a forum, an audience, and since she can't admit her real accomplishments—framing Devin and killing Jimmie—they agree she'll seek it elsewhere."

Victoria looked disgusted. "She killed off her only confidant. That's just poor planning."

Calla smiled. "They're also convinced she follows Peeps's column. Here's the article for this morning." She retrieve the newspaper from the counter behind her and tossed it on the table.

The New York Tattletale

TPIS (Thank Peeps It's Saturday)
by Peeps Galloway, Gossipmonger
(And proud of it!)

Darlings, it's *Saturday*. Need I say more?

Stick with me, Manhattanites, and I'll pull you out of the trenches of your cubicle-chained, humdrum life and show you what life in the city is all about—looking great, sizzling music, potent cocktails and blowing large amounts of dough.

While gorgeous detectives who were recently indicted are being questioned under hot lights about a certain murder (told you I'd get the scoop), you can show your support—or join in on his condemnation—with a drink at Urge. I certainly will.

Be sure to say hi if you see me.

Kidding! You know you won't actually see me. Tsk, tsk, dear followers, I have to go incognito as usual. I make the noble sacrifice for you. After all, how else will I know if Jenny Jam and Simon B. show up together, even though they supposedly had a public breakup over which rehab spa to enter after their North American tour is over?

Rest assured, all the *best* people will be out and about. I'll be trolling several hot spots, including Black Mask and Peel It!, but Urge is the final destination. I simply *adore* their cocktails with glowing neon ice cubes.

Ask for Mike behind the bar. He's been known to give a girl an extra shot with a wink.

Glowing as a cube,

—*Peeps*

P.S. My assistants and various members of my spy network will also be dashing about, so if you should encounter one, be as truthful as you dare. (How else will I know how to twist whatever you say into something more interesting and printable?)

"HOWARD IS AT THE STATION now, holed up in an interrogation room with Anderson and Reid to strategize ways to get the suspect to confess," Calla said when the group shifted their attention back to her.

"Talk about lousy assignments for a defense attorney." Victoria pointed at the column. "Mike?"

"Lieutenant Reid." Calla glanced at her watch. "He should be here anytime. One of Shelby's staff is going to show him the finer points of bartending."

Shelby looked skeptical. "I can't imagine Colin Reid tossing glasses about and flirting with women sidled up to the bar. Why don't we put Trevor and Jared behind the bar? Reid can pose as a bouncer."

"Or the manager," Victoria suggested.

Calla glanced at Devin, who said nothing. He was crazy about Calla, but no way was he jumping in to regarding her friends' role in the operation. "They can't pose as anything," Calla said, her voice surprisingly steady. "You guys aren't going to be there."

Shelby looked confused; Victoria narrowed her eyes

dangerously. Devin reached for another cookie and considered moving to the other side of the room.

Out of the line of fire.

"Aren't going to be where?" Victoria asked, her tone hard and cold as ice.

"At the nightclubs, on this mission, listening to Peeps babble incessantly or anywhere near a psycho killer," Calla said, obviously not nearly as intimidated by her friend as any other sensible, breathing person would be.

Shelby and Victoria exchanged a look. "Who votes for a change in gang leadership?" Shelby asked.

Everybody but Calla and Devin raised their hands.

"Excellent." Shelby smiled. "I nominate Victoria. Is there a second?"

"Seconded," Jared said.

"All in favor of Victoria as the new leader of the Robin Hood gang, bestowing her full powers of the office and offering her the final yea or veto on any mission engaged in by the gang, please vote now."

Again, all hands shot up except Calla's and Devin's.

"Four to two," Shelby said proudly. "Congratulations, Robin aka Victoria. Is there any other business?"

Devin hadn't had time to take more than a single bite of his cookie. "That happened fast."

Calla crossed her arms over her chest. "Your coup won't succeed. I'm the one with the inside track to the police."

"Is this your doing?" Victoria demanded, glaring at Devin.

"No." Devin put down his cookie. He was crazy about Calla—well, more than crazy if he was honest with himself—but if he'd learned anything in the past couple of weeks, it was the power of friendship. "You

think I'd let my girlfriend go undercover to catch a murderer, but I draw the line at her buddies helping?"

"You're not doing this without us," Victoria said.

Devin, knowing it was useless to disagree, kept quiet, knowing Calla would have her own opinions about wanting to protect her friends' safety.

"Reid's right," she said. "This is too dangerous. I don't want you there."

"You're not doing this without us," Trevor repeated.

Calla looked on the verge of screaming. "Devin, do something."

He shook his head. "You're the one who convinced me that I needed the gang. Why would I change my mind now?"

Seeing the angry, but fearful, expression on her face, he stood and took her into his arms. Devin wanted to be standing with her tonight more than he wanted to breathe, but not only couldn't they take the chance of the killer recognizing him, he was supposed to be worried about being arrested again, not out partying.

"I'm not happy about any of you risking yourselves for me, but when a fellow cop is threatened, team members suit up and volunteers stand in line. Isn't that the Robin Hood motto?"

Calla pursed her lips. "Maybe."

He trailed his fingers through her silky, golden hair, reminding himself he'd be only a few feet away from her the whole time. "The op has more protection than the Federal Reserve Bank. We can end this. Don't you want your friends there when we do?"

As soon as the words *end this* were out of his mouth, he wanted to recall them. Was he closing his case, or ending things with Calla?

"Fine," Calla said, "but I wanna be Robin again."

AFTER ENDURING TWO nightclubs full of blaring music, overpriced drinks and randy guys intent on picking up any female with a pulse, Calla slid onto a bar stool at Urge with a tired groan.

Why did undercover operatives on TV look like they were having so much fun? Hell, she usually had fun hanging out at energetic clubs.

But it was a whole different game when your lover's future was in jeopardy.

"Hey, beautiful. What'll you have?"

Hearing the familiar, deep voice, Calla nearly kissed Jared in gratitude. "You have no idea how glad I am to see you."

"At least he won't spend the next half hour trying to look down your shirt," Devin muttered via the earpiece she wore as part of the audio and video surveillance he and Detective Anderson were conducting from the van outside.

"I'll drink to that," Calla said. "Give me one of those glowing ice cube things. With booze this time."

She'd been ordering club soda and lime all night while watching seemingly everybody else in the city have a great time. She was so tense, she could drive nails with the heel of her hand. Convinced she was doing something wrong by not attracting their suspect, she glanced around.

There were plenty of blondes. But she only saw people enjoying themselves. People who were visiting on business or on vacation or fellow city-dwellers, who'd worked their butts of all week so they could keep their studio apartments and were thrilled to blow off stress on the dance floor, laughing with friends.

As she arrived, she'd seen Reid prowling the club, posing as an assistant manager and looking very much the part of the rule-following dictator, who might be eager to sell drinks, but wasn't going to let the fun get out of hand.

Perfect casting.

As were the roles of her fellow gang members, who enjoyed themselves with drinks and tapas in a nearby booth, even as their attention darted to her every few seconds.

"Ask Jared if there's any sign of the suspect," Devin prompted.

"Seen a champagne-drinking homicidal blonde?" she asked as Jared set her drink in front of her.

Jared briefly slid his hand over hers as he passed her an extra cocktail napkin. "Not so far. How's it going with Peeps?"

Calla recalled the conversation in the limo that Trevor had insisted they rent for the night.

"So you and the hot detective, huh?" Peeps had asked her, nudging her shoulder and winking.

Calla had continued staring at the passing lights of Manhattan. "If you think I'm telling you anything, you're out of your mind."

Now, with little effort, Calla could see the gossip-monger at the opposite end of the bar. She was chatting up a guy who looked amazingly like Jets linebacker Franko Ballinger. Probably was. That Peeps was strategic and shrewd.

Calla had taken a single sip of her drink when the amorous couple beside her shuffled off and someone else slid onto the stool next to her.

And her heart stuttered.

A skinny blonde with long hair, teased-at-the-crown, fashionably dressed and holding a glass of champagne, smiled at her. Even with the scent of booze, and various perfumes and colognes, the faint aroma of gardenias hovered in the air.

"You're one of Peeps Galloway's spies," the blonde said, her cold, steel-gray eyes meeting Calla's boldly.

Calla didn't have to fake her look of surprise. *It's her,* she thought and heard Devin's curse in her ears.

Knowing he was more tense than she was, considering who she was face-to-face with, Calla shoved her panic aside and pretended she was on stage, daftly claiming world peace was her goal in life. "I *wish*. Oh, my goodness. Isn't Peeps the absolute *best?*"

The blonde looked mildly disappointed. "She certainly delivers the best news."

Mustering both her anger and nerve, Calla held out her hand. "Rosie Savannah." At least she'd thought ahead about her pseudonym. Her real name had once been printed in Peeps's column, after all.

"Stephanie," the woman returned, shaking her hand then glancing away.

"Why do you think I work for Peeps?"

"I saw you come in with her."

So Peeps's identity wasn't as secret as she thought. Yet another exaggeration. Calla shouldn't have been surprised.

"I *do* work for Peeps," Calla whispered, leaning toward her mark and hoping she didn't have a heroin syringe concealed in her tiny cocktail bag that she might unexpectedly jab her with. "Don't tell." She giggled out of sheer nervousness but hoped her reaction would be mistaken for Peeps-like enthusiasm.

Stephanie's head whipped round in Calla's direction. "No kidding?"

Calla proudly held up the glowing cocktail in front of her. "I'm only a small cog in the glamorous wheel, of course, but I like to think I play a real part in making things happen."

"I'm sure you do, darling," Stephanie said, somehow condescending and complimentary at the same time.

No wonder the crazy chick had charmed Jimmie—and who knew who else. Unfortunately, Calla's instinct was to smack her.

Thankfully, big, strong, charming Jared saved her.

"Can I get you a refill, beautiful?" he asked, planting his hand, attached to his muscular arm, which led to his tan face and winning smile, on the bar in front of Stephanie.

Devin aside, Stephanie wasn't immune to an easy-on-the-eyes man. She drained her glass, then held out the empty crystal. "Champagne, Veuve Clicquot."

"Right away."

Jared shifted away, though Calla was comforted that he didn't move far.

"See that dweeby-looking guy at the table on the left side of the bar?" Stephanie asked.

Calla swung her gaze that way and sipped her drink to cover her cough. It was Howard. She realized instantly that he'd been thrown in to knock both her and Stephanie off balance. "Yeah."

"That's Howard Bleaker. He's a defense attorney."

"Really?"

"The cop he's defending arrested my brother five years ago."

Calla fought to remember if a sister named Stephanie was in their files. She wasn't on the list of interviewees who'd originally been scheduled. But since she could hardly say that, she repeated, "Really?"

Stephanie tossed back her fresh glass of champagne

like a shot. "He died in prison six months ago. Cops are all scum. They're all scum."

If Calla had any doubt that Stephanie was their killer, it was wiped away by that single statement. Her stomach burned as she tried to hold to her cover story, plus, she was ticked the cops had thrown Howard in. Everybody she loved was within twenty feet of this delusional murderer, and Calla was the one responsible for pulling them into this circle.

"I heard he's been arrested," she managed to say to Stephanie. "You think all cops are bad like that?"

"Well, this one is." Stephanie's eyes gleamed. "Course he's not a cop at all now."

No, he certainly wasn't, and the chance to make things right burned in Calla's heart, as she sat inches away from the woman who'd caused all this misery.

At the same time it occurred to her that Stephanie had admitted nothing that couldn't be spun as mere alcohol-induced ranting. Nothing that actually connected her to the murder, other than instinct and gardenias. Or maybe the glass Jared had taken and skillfully set aside for the crime lab.

They needed more.

Calla needed more than justice. She wanted revenge.

"No, Devin's not a cop," she said, pushing off her bar stool to stand. "He should be, but, thanks to you, he's not."

The befuddled expression on Stephanie's face was almost worth all the turmoil and uncertainty.

Calla realized this single moment was why cops worked for less pay and little appreciation, why they strapped on weapons and vests, fully acknowledging the risk they could be injured or killed. They patrolled the streets of cities and towns. They sat in vans and cars, listening for slip-ups among real, criminal gangs, hoping to get a lead on how to disrupt what the bad guys were planning. They readily accepted the challenge of chasing some idiot robber ten blocks in order to keep him from doing so again.

The system of law and order had its flaws, and justice needed a nudge every now and then, but there were amazing men and women who sought to balance the scales each and every day, and when you worked outside the system to extract revenge, you invited arbitrary retribution. No single person should avenge. Maybe not even a well-meaning gang.

Robin had served a great cause, but she—they—had to retire.

"You killed Jimmie Forrester," she said, proud of herself for her casual tone.

Choking on her drink, Stephanie rose, and Calla was certain she was going to run. She didn't touch her, though, as Devin had warned in her ear.

"I have no idea what you're talking about," Stephanie said boldly, her eyes turning arctic.

Calla ground her teeth as she dug for the effort to stay in control. "Oh, yes, you do. Your brother got arrested, and you got mad." Calla shrugged. "You can't imagine in the last few days how many women I've talked to who think like you do."

"Like we've all talked to," Victoria said.

Though Calla didn't dare take her attention off the desperate woman in front of her, she felt her friends close behind her. "I'm sorry about your brother, but what you've done isn't justice. It's just plain wrong."

"We've got your back, baby," Devin said in her ear.

Calla shuddered, knowing, at long last, that it was time to confess. "You might have loved your brother, but I love Devin Antonio. You challenged the wrong vengeful blonde, honey."

Fueled by hate and whatever else she held against her cold heart, Stephanie charged Calla, attempting to get her hands around her neck.

Calla whipped out her leg in a kick her daddy would have been pleased with.

As Stephanie's body crumbled at Calla's feet and her friends huddled closer and others rushed in from every entrance of the club. Calla noticed Peeps's gleeful expression out of the corner of her eye.

Oh, well, they couldn't prevent every injustice.

Maybe, though, after tonight, her gang wouldn't appear in the papers quite so much.

The next thing she knew, she was in Devin's arms. "We got her," he said, holding her tight. "I can never repay you."

She didn't expect payment. She expected him.

Leaning back, she didn't like the relieved but distant look in his eyes. She knew he was in work-mode, but something wasn't right. "I need you."

He kissed her, then offered a strained smile as he helped his colleagues lead the suspect out of the club in handcuffs.

And she knew it was finally over.

15

STEPHANIE PILAR, who had a diagnosed mental condition, and who had been in therapy with her ultimate victim Jimmie Forrester, was behind bars.

Hopefully, Calla thought, *for good.*

Her prints matched the partials the cops had pulled from the flower arrangement in Jimmie's apartment, and she had not only gardenia-ladened perfumes on her bathroom counter, she had a chemistry set in which she'd tried to extract the essence of the blossoms for her own, personal scent.

Her stepbrother, once employed as a gardener, had been caught in the act and arrested by Devin for armed robbery. Sadly, he'd died in prison in a gang stabbing.

Ever since Robin Hood had been officially disbanded a week ago, Calla didn't like to think about the notion of a gang. Or the fact that a row of gardenia bushes thrived in front of Stephanie's Brooklyn cottage.

As for how Devin was coping with getting his badge back and the assault charges dismissed, Calla had no idea.

She hadn't talked to or seen him since Stephanie's arrest.

He wouldn't answer calls or texts. He wasn't at home—or pretended not to be. The NYPD refused to let her beyond the reception desk, claiming the investigation was over, and the officers needed seclusion to finish their case reports.

Her declaration of love over official police channels was probably too much for him to handle.

Her friends—the former gang—had embraced her as expected, but as comforted as she was, she found herself clinging to Sharky.

The cat understood both her affection and irritation. Lonely, they slept together. By day, they vowed to forget him.

She was right back where she started, chasing a man who didn't want her. She got it, he wasn't a schmaltzy hearts and flowers kind of guy, which was fine by her. When he wasn't being a stubborn hermit, she liked him as he was. When had she ever indicated otherwise?

But she wanted to change one thing. She wanted to love him. If only he'd let her.

"You do not have good luck with women."

A romance critique from Howard? Devin figured he could do worse. He hadn't even had the guts to actually break up with Calla. He'd simply avoided her, knowing she'd be furious and toss him away.

"I mean, you have the cool job and the good looks," Howard went on, "but you are doomed, my friend."

Hunched over glasses of whiskey at O'Leary's, Devin and Howard were lone wolves. Devin now had *two* homicidal women in his past; Howard was despondent over his prospects for the future.

As they both knew their crucial loss of Calla, they had only each other.

During the rush and confusion of Jimmie's killer's arrest, Devin had never gotten around to asking Jared and Trevor for advice in the romance department. And while he imagined Calla had celebrated with her friends, Devin had stayed away.

Avoidance was instinctive.

Thanks to desk work and sorting out the procedure for getting his badge back, he figured he'd sounded plausible for a few hours. But the more hours that went by, the more certain he was that he was doing the right thing by keeping his distance.

She didn't belong with him.

She was light and hope; he was shadow and uncertainty. He'd known that from the moment he'd met her all those months ago. Nothing had changed. If anything, his suspension had magnified their differences.

He was grateful, and always would be, but since vigilante justice had been used against them and Calla had declared Robin Hood retired, he saw no point in continuing the fairy tale.

"Men always want to be a woman's first love— women like to be a man's last romance."

On the verge of sipping from his glass, Devin paused to consider Howard's words. "What the hell are you talking about?"

"Oscar Wilde," Howard said, shaking his head ruefully. "It's no wonder you're alone."

"*You're* alone."

"But I don't have to be." Howard leaned back in his chair. "I mention I'm a lawyer working with the top cops in the city, and I'd have twenty women lined up to talk to me."

"Uh-huh. And how many of them would want you

to get their lover-husband-brother-uncle off of whatever he's currently charged with?

"Cops are mean."

Satisfied he'd burst somebody else's bubble, Devin nodded. "And don't you forget it, buddy."

They drank in silence for a few minutes before Devin admitted to himself he needed Howard. Which is one of the reasons he'd asked his former attorney to meet him in the first place. Why was he determined to alienate the people who got close?

He'd been determined not to repeat his parents' mistakes, yet, here he was being a completely ignorant jerk. "You're a better boyfriend than me," he confessed, fighting not to choke on the words.

"I'm—" Thankfully, Howard's brilliant mind skipped over the segue, not to mention the obvious jokes, and nodded. "Have you tried telling her you love her?"

"No."

"Oh, good grief."

"You're better at words."

Howard shook his head. "I'm not telling you what to say."

"I'm not a schmaltzy hearts and flowers guy."

Howard looked surprised. "No kidding?"

Devin stared into the depths of his whiskey, but the color was too dark to compare to Calla. "She's so… golden. Like a star around the moon. She lights up everybody around her, and my life, my past, my job is all about despair and darkness. But, for some crazy reason, she believes in me as nobody ever has. I don't think I can live without her."

"Not bad words," Howard commented.

"Ramblings," Devin argued.

"A bit." Howard shrugged. "Remember the moon

wouldn't shine so brightly without the the dark, end-less sky to reflect a distinction."

"Wilde, again?"

"No. Howard Bleaker." Smiling, he signaled for the check. "Be a hearts and flowers guy, my friend, and live the fairy tale."

CALLA COULDN'T IMAGINE who was knocking on her door at nine-thirty on a Sunday. Chinese food had al-ready been delivered, and she'd told her friends that she needed to work, since she had a story due on Wednes-day, which she hadn't started to write.

Of course the cursor on her laptop was blinking like a bomb, and she hadn't typed a word, but she hadn't thought about Devin in the past ten minutes, either.

Damn.

There went her record.

She scooped up Sharky and strode down the hall. Peeking through the hole in her door, she swore coarsely enough to pin Sharky's ears back.

"I know I deserve that," Devin called from the other side.

"You're damned right you do," Calla called back, feeling like an idiot.

"Any chance you'll let me in to explain?" he asked. "Your neighbors are liable to call the cops."

She longed to kick the door, but she'd bruised her toe when she'd taken her anger out on the dishwasher. "You *are* the cops."

"Thanks to you."

With a huff of reluctance, she unlocked the door, then immediately walked away, dropping onto the liv-ing room sofa. "You've made it perfectly clear you don't want anything to do with me," she said, glaring at him as he stood in front of her.

Which is when she saw him holding a dozen roses and a heart-shaped box of candy.

Sharky, the little traitor, purred like crazy.

"What—"

"I'm an idiot."

"You are?" *Yes, he is,* her conscience reminded her.

"Can I sit?" he asked.

In a daze, she nodded, watching him set the hearts and flowers on the coffee table.

Tentatively, he reached out with his hand and covered hers. "I never believed I deserved you, and maybe I still don't, but Howard reminded me that for the moon to shine, it needs a dark sky, so maybe we need each other." He shook his head. "No, not maybe, I need you. Always."

"Howard?" she asked, confused.

Devin laughed and leaned forward, cupping her face in his palm. "Not exactly the name I was looking for." He stroked her cheek several times, sending tingles of desire straight through her. "I love you. Always."

Her gaze searched his, and though hurt and doubt lingered, Devin knew he'd do anything to make sure she understood how genuine his words truly were.

"And I love you," she said.

He pressed his lips against hers. Relief, like rain after a long drought, washed over him. "So I heard in the surveillance truck."

"Sorry, I sort of blurted it out."

"I'm glad somebody had the guts to." And he might never fully understand why she cherished him so much, but he was through rejecting the blessings in his life. He hadn't been born under a bright star, but he was sailing by its light from now on. "I needed help from Howard."

She glanced at the table. "Hearts and flowers?"

"You deserve them." He squeezed her hand. "I'd be lost without you."

"I disbanded the gang."

"I heard. I have to admit I'm happy. I'd rather not listen to you confront a killer anytime soon."

Her fingertips traced a path down his shoulder. "I've had enough adventure for the time being."

Moving Sharky to the floor, Devin pinned her against the sofa cushions and inhaled her sweetness as he trailed kisses along her neck, her jaw, her lips. Nothing would ever feel so amazing as her smile and dedication.

"Nothing happens on Sunday night," she whispered.

He grinned against her silky skin. "It does in fairy tales."

* * * * *

COMING NEXT MONTH from Harlequin® Blaze™
AVAILABLE SEPTEMBER 18, 2012

#711 BLAZING BEDTIME STORIES, VOLUME IX
Bedtime Stories
Rhonda Nelson and Karen Foley
Two of Harlequin Blaze's bestselling authors invite you to curl up in bed with their latest collection of sensual fairy tales, guaranteed to inspire sweet—and *very* sexy—dreams!

#712 THE MIGHTY QUINNS: CAMERON
The Mighty Quinns
Kate Hoffmann
Neither Cameron Quinn nor FBI agent Sophie Reyes is happy hanging out in Vulture Creek, New Mexico. But when Cameron helps Sophie on a high profile case, he realizes that sexy Sophie has stolen his heart.

#713 OWN THE NIGHT
Made in Montana
Debbi Rawlins
Jaded New Yorker Alana Richardson wants to go a little country with Blackfoot Falls sheriff Noah Calder. He just needs to figure out if she belongs in his bed...or in jail!

#714 FEELS SO RIGHT
Friends With Benefits
Isabel Sharpe
Physical therapist Demi Anderson knows she has the right job when the world's sexiest man walks into her studio, takes off his shirt and begs her to help him. Colin Russo needs Demi's healing touch...but having her hands on him is sweet torture!

#715 LIVING THE FANTASY
Kathy Lyons
Ali Flores has never believed in luck, until she accidentally lands a par on a video game tour. Now she's learning all about gaming. But what she *really* likes is playing with hunky company CEO Ken Johnson....

#716 FOLLOW MY LEAD
Stepping Up
Lisa Renee Jones
The host and one of the judges of TV's hottest reality dance show put the past behind them and embark on a sensually wild, emotionally charged fling!

You can find more information on upcoming Harlequin® titles, free excerpts and more at www.Harlequin.com.

HBCNM09

REQUEST YOUR FREE BOOKS!
2 FREE NOVELS PLUS 2 FREE GIFTS!

Harlequin® *Blaze*™

red-hot reads!

YES! Please send me 2 FREE Harlequin® Blaze™ novels and my 2 FREE gifts (gifts are worth about $10). After receiving them, if I don't wish to receive any more books, I can return the shipping statement marked "cancel." If I don't cancel, I will receive 6 brand-new novels every month and be billed just $4.49 per book in the U.S. or $4.96 per book in Canada. That's a saving of at least 14% off the cover price. It's quite a bargain. Shipping and handling is just 50¢ per book in the U.S. and 75¢ per book in Canada.* I understand that accepting the 2 free books and gifts places me under no obligation to buy anything. I can always return a shipment and cancel at any time. Even if I never buy another book, the two free books and gifts are mine to keep forever.

151/351 HDN FEQE

Name _____ (PLEASE PRINT) _____

Address _____ Apt. # _____

City _____ State/Prov. _____ Zip/Postal Code _____

Signature (if under 18, a parent or guardian must sign) _____

Mail to the **Reader Service:**
IN U.S.A.: P.O. Box 1867, Buffalo, NY 14240-1867
IN CANADA: P.O. Box 609, Fort Erie, Ontario L2A 5X3

Not valid for current subscribers to Harlequin Blaze books.

Want to try two free books from another line?
Call 1-800-873-8635 or visit www.ReaderService.com.

* Terms and prices subject to change without notice. Prices do not include applicable taxes. Sales tax applicable in N.Y. Canadian residents will be charged applicable taxes. Offer not valid in Quebec. This offer is limited to one order per household. All orders subject to credit approval. Credit or debit balances in a customer's account(s) may be offset by any other outstanding balance owed by or to the customer. Please allow 4 to 6 weeks for delivery. Offer available while quantities last.

Your Privacy—The Reader Service is committed to protecting your privacy. Our Privacy Policy is available online at www.ReaderService.com or upon request from the Reader Service.

We make a portion of our mailing list available to reputable third parties that offer products we believe may interest you. If you prefer that we not exchange your name with third parties, or if you wish to clarify or modify your communication preferences, please visit us at www.ReaderService.com/consumerchoice or write to us at Reader Service Preference Service, P.O. Box 9062, Buffalo, NY 14269. Include your complete name and address.

HBI1B

New York Times *bestselling author Brenda Jackson
presents TEXAS WILD,
a brand-new Westmoreland novel.*

Available October 2012 from Harlequin Desire®!

Rico figured there were a lot of things in life he didn't
know. But the one thing he did know was that there was no
way Megan Westmoreland was going to Texas with him.
He was attracted to her, big-time, and had been from the
moment he'd seen her at Micah's wedding four months ago.
Being alone with her in her office was bad enough. But
the idea of them sitting together on a plane or in a car was
rousing him just thinking about it.

He could tell by the mutinous expression on her face that
he was in for a fight. That didn't bother him. Growing up,
he'd had two younger sisters to deal with, so he knew well
how to handle a stubborn female.

She crossed her arms over her chest. "Other than the fact
that you prefer working alone, give me another reason I
can't go with you."

He crossed his arms over his own chest. "I don't need
another reason. You and I talked before I took this case, and
I told you I would get you the information you wanted…
doing things my way."

He watched as she nibbled on her bottom lip. So now she
was remembering. Good. Even so, he couldn't stop looking
into her beautiful dark eyes, meeting her fiery gaze head-on.

"As the client, I demand that you take me," she said.

He narrowed his gaze. "You can demand all you want,
but you're not going to Texas with me."

Megan's jaw dropped. "I *will* be going with you sinc
there's no good reason that I shouldn't."

He didn't say anything for a moment. "Okay, there
another reason I won't take you with me. One that you'd d
well to consider," he said in a barely controlled tone. Sh
had pushed him, and he didn't like being pushed.

"Fine, let's hear it," she snapped furiously.

He placed his hands in the pockets of his jeans, stoc
with his legs braced apart and leveled his gaze on he
"I want you, Megan. Bad. And if you go anywhere with m
I'm going to have you."

He then turned and walked out of her office.

Will Megan go to Texas with Rico?

*Find out in Brenda Jackson's brand-new
Westmoreland novel, TEXAS WILD.*

Available October 2012 from Harlequin Desire®.

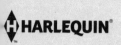

Calla plopped the rest of the plates in the dishwasher and slammed the door. "Maybe the thief had a partner, and he didn't want to split the booty, so he clobbered his buddy and took off."

"The booty?"

She let out a huff as she marched toward him, wondering if it was possible his head injury had made him even more difficult than normal. "Loot, plunder, goods, ill-gotten gains. Pick your term. I've got a thesaurus on the bookshelf that'll help you find dozens more if you like."

"Seems like a lot of effort for one purse."

Calla flopped on the sofa. "You're sure it wasn't there when you woke up?"

"I don't think so, but I was pretty groggy."

"And yet you managed to call for help."

"An obvious flaw in the logic of this guy's story. I'm the one who called the ambulance. Why would I do that if I'd gone to all the trouble to kick the crap out of him?"

"None of this makes sense. We need to find you a lawyer." She picked up her phone from the coffee table in front of her. "I'll call Victoria. Her dad's bound to know somebody."

"We?" Devin stopped pacing and shook his head, which he obviously regretted, because he winced, pressing his fingertips to his temples. "I appreciate you helping me out last night, but I'll handle things from here."

"Unlike the NYPD, I am standing by you. You need help."

"I can take care of myself." He must have realized she'd debunked that statement pretty soundly over the past twelve hours, since he added, "Usually. I don't need your gang."

She scowled. "We're not a gang."

"So you keep saying. Look, I should go."

As he headed toward the hallway, she stepped in front of him. "Don't. Let me help you. It's the least my friends and I can do after all the times you've rescued us."

He narrowed his eyes. "I don't need rescuing."

The man was pricklier than a desert cactus. "Stay."

"No."

"I'd threaten to hold your pain meds hostage, but you'd probably dip into the whiskey bottle again."

"I think I'll lay off the whiskey for a while."

"Wise idea. You can't go home, somebody tried to kill you."

"A bump on the head isn't a near-death experience."

"But whoever hit you and the guy you chased is out there. What if he comes looking for you?"

Devin laid his hand on his side, where he usually carried his pistol. By the expression on his face, she could tell he wasn't happy by its absence.

"Us regular folks can't carry a gun in the city," she reminded him.

"They took my badge, too."

There was a world of frustration in those five simple words. Though he wasn't big on sharing, she knew he defined himself by his job. The possibility of losing it was no doubt terrifying.

Counting on rejection, but past caring, she grasped his hand. "I'm sorry. I'll help you get it back."

He looked, not at her, but their joined hands. "I appreciate the offer, but I have to handle this alone."

"Why?"

His gaze moved to hers. "It's my problem."

"There's no weakness in accepting help from a

friend," she said gently, sensing he was on the verge of bolting.

"And we're friends."

"Aren't we?"

His bright green eyes stood out starkly from his tanned skin. People of Irish and Italian decent really should mate more often if this was the result. Her friends thought he was gorgeous, but dark and rough. She saw him as wounded and lonely. He spoke to her on an elemental level, and deeper feelings were undeniably lurking.

Feelings he seemed determined to ignore or deny.

"I thought so," she said finally to his question about friendship.

"Are we more than friends?"

Her heart gave a swift kick to her ribs. "Pardon me?"

"We didn't..." He trailed off and clearly struggled to continue. She wondered if he was even aware he was stroking the back of her hand with his thumb. "I mean, I didn't...do anything with you last night, did I?"

There'd been some clumsy passes, of course, but they, unfortunately, meant nothing. Was that what he was talking about? In his case, *thing* could mean something as monumental as having a conversation for more than two minutes. "Do what kind of thing?"

"I woke up naked."

Her face turned pink. "I thought you'd be more comfortable out of your clothes." He did more for a black T-shirt and jeans than anybody she knew, but the view beneath the cotton was exponentially better. Not that she'd looked. For long. She cleared her throat. "I was expecting some kind of undergarment, actually. Do you always...?"

"No. I need to do laundry."

"Ah. And the scar on your hip?"

"I got stabbed."

He gave the explanation with the same casual tone that most people used for "I think I'll have fries with my burger," intriguing and mystifying her more than ever.

And he was still caressing her hand. She inched toward him. Yes, he was injured, confused, weak and needy—even if he didn't want to admit he was. It would be wrong, very wrong, to take advantage of him in his current state.

And yet her libido was also needy and it was whispering seductively about the possibility of this being her one and only opportunity with him. She'd been crushing on him for six months. Other than the head wound plus alcohol fiasco of the night before, he seemed determined not to make the first move. *Any* move, actually.

Yet, somewhere, somewhere way deep down, she sensed he needed her with the same intensity.

Texans were nothing if not determined and resilient. She certainly knew how to take control. And she had a much better weapon than a firearm.

Before her conscience could talk sense into her, or he could think quickly enough to shove her away, she wrapped her arms around his neck and pressed her lips to his.

Desperate as the move was, it was worth the reward.

He crushed her against him, bracing his hand at the back of her head to hold her in place as he drove his tongue past her lips. Her senses ignited, and he fanned the flames, consuming her like a man starved for air.

Finally was all she could think. Finally he'd let go of the tight rein he held on his control.

She embraced his heat, his aggression and need. Ev-

erything about him enticed her to learn more, to be drawn further into the inferno. Why was he so determined to be alone? What had made him so cynical and stony? Why did she want so badly to find out if anything soft lingered beneath?

As the thought occurred, his touch turned gentle. His hand, braced at the small of her back, slid around her waist, glided down her hip. If he tugged the ties of her robe, she'd be standing before him in nothing but panties and a camisole, but he seemed more interested in her mouth.

Dreams she'd had alone in her bed, in the dead of night rushed back. How often had she woken in a sweat, so sure he'd been with her between the sheets, positive she smelled his cologne on her skin, only to find herself alone and aching instead?

Fantasies never lived up to their impossible promises, yet she continued to hope and wonder. Now she finally had him.

I dream of you day and night.

Had he felt the same? Had he longed for her, too? Would this disastrous frame-up bring them together in a way their past connections hadn't been able to?

He pushed her away roughly and suddenly, and she glimpsed the fire in his eyes seconds before he spun with a muttered "sorry" before he stalked down the hall, slamming the door behind him.

Breathing hard, Calla stood rigid where he'd left her. Most of her questions were still frustratingly unanswered. She knew he wanted her, but he refused to give into that need. She intended to find out why.

Because friendship was far from the only thing she wanted.

"OKAY, GIRLS," CALLA said to her best buds via her laptop's video link. "I've got a serious problem here."

"Let me guess," Victoria began, then sipped from a coffee mug while the window at her back exhibited a collection of Manhattan high-rises. "Antonio's in a bad mood."

Shelby, the Swiss Alps at her back, frowned, her normally golden-hazel eyes dark with concern. "Is he okay, Calla? Why didn't he come to the wedding?"

"It's a big, damn mess."

Calla told her friends the abbreviated version of assault, frame-up and suspension. "We've got to help him."

"Certainly we will," Shelby said immediately.

"Does he want us to help him?" Victoria asked. "Antonio doesn't seem like the needy type."

"He needs us," Calla insisted, though she knew Victoria was right. "He's concussed and suspended."

"And angry, I'll bet," Victoria added.

Calla bit her lip. "Actually, he raced out of here, slamming the door behind him, about five minutes ago." She paused, taking care not to look her friends' directly in the eye. "Course that might have been because I kissed him."

"Well, that would—" Shelby leaned forward. "You kissed him?"

"It's about damn time" was Victoria's dry comment.

"How did it happen?" Shelby asked.

"He was feeling guilty because he couldn't remember if we'd slept together or not, and he was holding my hand, which, in retrospect, I don't think he realized he was doing, and all these feelings welled up inside me—"

Victoria held up her hand. "Hold it. He couldn't remember if you'd had sex?"

"He was pretty out of it last night," Calla said.

"Apparently," Victoria remarked.

"So, anyway," Calla went on, "I laid one on him, and he seemed really into it, then he suddenly darted out the door."

Victoria shook her head. "I've said it once, I'll say it again—that guy has issues."

"You're not being helpful, V," Shelby said before she directed her gaze to Calla. "He's not thinking straight. That's why he pushed you away. If you want to help him, you'll have to be persistent. Think of him as an exclusive interview you absolutely have to get."

Victoria gestured with her mug. "Gotta agree with you there."

Calla made an effort not to pout, but it was tough. "He's been doing a pretty good job of avoiding me the last six months."

"But he *does* want you," Shelby said, clearly frustrated. "Anybody can see it. Your timing was just wrong. The first move has got to be perfect."

"He made plenty of moves last night," Calla said. "But since he was toasted, I don't think those count."

"Sure they do," Shelby insisted. "His inhibitions were down, so he went with his unvarnished instincts. Be persistent. And when I get home, we'll triple-team him." She paused. "No way will this trumped-up assault charge last."

Calla knew she'd made the right move by calling her friends, even if she had interrupted Shelby's honeymoon. "I could use the backup. In the meantime, he's going to need a good attorney. V, can you call your dad for a recommendation?"

Victoria nodded. "I'll ask, and I'm sure he knows somebody, but he'll be expensive."

Calla winced. "I don't think Devin will have the budget for a highflier."

"What about that guy you took to V's Christmas party last year?" Shelby asked.

Victoria scowled. "The one who kept drooling on her rhinestone shoes?"

"That's him," Shelby said, undeterred. "Didn't he leave the public defender's office to open his own practice?"

"Howard?" Calla asked. "I don't know. He asked me to marry him on our second date. It took a long time to let him down gently."

"Speaking of proposals..." Shelby grinned. "How are things with you and Jared, Victoria?"

"Fine," Victoria said. "No proposals. We agreed."

Over Labor Day weekend, Victoria had fallen in love with a Montana adventurer. Though wild about her new man, she was also wildly independent and seemed to be struggling with the concept of coupledom.

Victoria shrugged, though her eyes were bright with lust. "In between him dragging me off to Turks and Caicos, we're—"

"He *drags* you off to Turks and Caicos?" Shelby interrupted in disbelief.

"Not exactly." Victoria's face actually turned pink. "But we go. In between we're trying to merge our apartments in the city. No easy task, as it turns out. He wants to buy the place next door, so we can knock out a wall, and he can build a man-cave where he can watch football and drink beer. But I remind him that I should have a chick-den where I can do hair and invite over gay guys to give me grooming tips."

"Who wins?" Calla asked.

"Nobody," Victoria said. "We argue, have sex then forget what we were arguing about."

"Sounds like a good thing," Calla muttered. "Shelby, does Trevor have a man-cave?"

"He has an office. With a minifridge stocked full of sparking water and champagne. I don't think cavemen ever envisioned the English aristocracy. His decorator's excellent, though. Course she makes in a month what I do in a year, but our place is beautiful, and she had a commercial-grade Sub-Zero fridge installed in the kitchen, so she's good in my book."

"Is her brother, sister, mother, father, cousin or next-door neighbor a lawyer?" Calla asked, wondering how they'd wandered into this tangent.

"Sorry." Shelby cleared her throat. "Back to Detective Antonio…does this suspension have anything to do with his trouble years ago?"

"I don't know," Calla admitted.

"You're going to have to ask him about it," Victoria reminded her.

Calla waved her hand. "Yeah, yeah. I will." And wouldn't *that* be fun? But if she was going to help, she had to have all the facts, no matter how painful.

"It seems to me we need to find out how strong the case is against him," Shelby said, echoing Calla's concern.

"And who's this witness accusing him of assault?" Victoria asked. "Antonio might be moody, but he wouldn't beat up some random stranger. Why would he need to? He probably intimidates most criminals with a single cold stare."

"The department isn't saying diddly," Calla said, knowing they had to find a way around that. Legal advice was imperative. Course he hadn't actually been

charged with anything…yet. If she hadn't seen the lost and furious expression on Devin's face, she'd wonder if she was overreacting. "Devin seems to think his boss believes in him, but he has to follow procedure. IAB's going to get involved." She paused to gather her emotions before she added, "They took his badge. I mean physically forced him to hand it over. Talk about humiliating."

Shelby's eyes darkened. "Oh, Calla."

Calla swallowed the lump in her throat. "It's not just what he does, it's who he is."

"He's still a cop," Victoria pointed out, pragmatic as always. "He has friends, right? You know, really stoic and tolerant ones. We obviously need somebody on the inside."

The contrast of Victoria's sarcasm brought back Calla's optimism. They had much more on their side than entrapment and lies. "He has friends." Though that was also wrapped up in hope, since she'd never met any of them. "I'll get him working on that angle right away. As soon as I find him," she muttered.

Victoria sighed in disgust. "Don't find him. He'll come to you."

Calla ground her teeth. "Sure he will."

"Bet," Victoria said, her eyes gleaming. "I got twenty on the Calla-dazzled detective."

"Calla-dazzled?" Shelby asked. "Is that a word?"

"It is now," Victoria asserted.

"Darling, we have dinner reservations," Calla heard Trevor, Shelby's new husband, say in his elegant English accent.

"I'm coming," Shelby called. "Say hi to Calla and Victoria."

Trevor's handsome face appeared in the video frame. "Good evening, ladies."

Calla had to suppress a sigh at his wavy black hair and vivid dark blue eyes. She really was desperate if she was lusting after her best friend's husband.

When he moved out of view, Calla got a glimpse of him walking away, dressed in a tailored charcoal suit. With this whole assault and suspension mess, she'd also missed out on seeing Devin in a suit at the wedding.

Infuriated again, Calla vowed to personally see that lying, purse-snatching jerk paid for that crime alone.

"How's the snow?" Calla whispered to Shelby as Trevor left the room.

"How's the sex?" Victoria asked at the same time.

"Great and great," Shelby returned. "And I need to get back to both. Trevor's patient as a saint, of course, but an emergency video chat with my girlfriends is enough to drive any groom to frustration."

"Thanks for the pep talk," Calla said. "Both of you."

"Tell Devin I'll make him some of my special cookies when I get back," Shelby said. "My next catering gig isn't for a while."

"And if he decides to blow off the NYPD and these bogus charges," Victoria added, "I'm sure Jared would be glad to take him off to Borneo or somewhere equally unextraditable."

Calla's throat tightened. "You guys are the best. Coffee's on me next week."

Victoria's lips winged up. "Wedding pictures and a plan to clear a friend on an assault charge. Only the three of us could have a coffee date like that."

After they signed off, Calla slumped on the sofa. Her and her buddies' latest adventures had included sending a fraudulent investor to prison and solving the theft

of a cursed multimillion-dollar diamond-and-sapphire necklace.

How hard could it be to convince the NYPD of the innocence of their determined, clever, though admittedly irascible, friend? Possibly without said friend's help?

She closed her laptop and leaned her head back. Who was she kidding? For months she'd lived in a fantasy world concerning Devin. The text, the craziness of last night and the impulsive kiss were all she had as any kind of evidence that he might want her, too.

And all of those events could be attributed to some sort of altered state.

He always comes to the rescue when you call him.

Super. If only she were the one suspended and accused of assault.

Maybe he was right. Maybe she should back out and let him deal with his problems on his own.

He'd never desert you.

Frustrated with the whole mess, and especially her interfering conscience, she rose. She needed a strong cup of tea and a big piece of leftover wedding cake.

On the way to the kitchen, she glanced at the plastic pharmacy bottle sitting on the counter. His pain meds.

Victoria was right. He'd be back.

Unless he found a liquor store open on Sundays.

4

DEVIN SHIFTED HIS WEIGHT and stared at the carpeted floor outside Calla's apartment.

He was never indecisive. What was wrong with him?

A head injury was too convenient to blame. Embarrassment over his suspension was whiney. Overwhelmed by a beautiful woman's kiss was damned humiliating.

That left regret.

But his DNA didn't include contrition. His personal motto was trudge on and forward and forget the crappy past that couldn't be changed.

Her touch and scent lingered on his skin. Weak and dizzy, he longed to give into the comfort she'd offered. To bury himself in her body, hold her against him beneath cool sheets, feel her breath heave, her pulse gather speed.

But she was too pure and perfect for him. He'd taint her somehow. He came from bad stock and had no doubt of a golden upbringing for her that included luxuries like regular meals and consistent lighting and heat. He imagined her dad as some big guy with a Stetson, a firm hand, but broad smile for his beauty queen daughter.

His old man had done a dime for armed robbery, and Devin hadn't seen him since he'd mooched four hundred bucks and taken off for parts unknown eight years ago.

He leaned his head against her door, bracing himself. He'd mistakenly given into his urges once before. The results hadn't been pretty.

Added to those crappy memories was the incessant pounding in his head. He wasn't thinking straight, and only Calla held the relief he needed—in more ways than one. He was weak and, for once, he needed somebody to share the burden.

Acknowledging he'd been stalling, he knocked on the door.

She answered wearing jeans, a gray sweater and a scowl.

"I shouldn't have taken off so abruptly," he said in a rush.

She raised her eyebrows. "That's almost an apology."

Was he really such an ass to her? Uncomfortable with the idea, he shifted his weight. "Sorry. I did—do appreciate your help."

"Uh-huh. Did you also suddenly remember I have your pain pills?"

He winced. "That crossed my mind."

After a lengthy pause, she opened the door wide. "Damned if I don't owe Victoria twenty bucks."

"I haven't forgotten I owe you for last night," he said as he closed the door behind him.

"You've bailed me and my friends out of several messes the last few months." She shook two white tablets out of the prescription bottle she scooped off the kitchen counter and handed them to him with a glass of water. "I think we can call it even."

He swallowed the pills, though he knew the medicine

would muddle his thoughts. Anything was better than the jackhammer that seemed to have taken up permanent residence between his ears.

She sat on the sofa and picked up a legal pad from the coffee table. "So who wants to frame you?" she asked, all business.

He sat beside her, keeping a safe distance. The last thing his confused brain needed was more kissing, though from her tone so far he guessed he'd blown another chance anyway. "Who doesn't? I've arrested a lot of people over the last fifteen years."

Her pen poised, she rolled her eyes. "Specifics, Detective. Names, dates, circumstances."

"That'll take days."

"You've got other plans?"

He peeked at the pad and saw it contained a record of everything that had happened the night before, along with times and locations. "Case notes? That's something cops do."

"It's what writers do, too. So spill."

"I've been involved with hundreds, maybe thousands of busts. I'll need access to the files at the department."

"What's the chance of Meyer letting you do that?"

"Zero."

"You've got friends inside the department, right? Somebody who can pass on information, give us details about the case against you?"

He shook his head. "I doubt anyone would risk their own job to break the law and help me. I wouldn't ask them to."

"You don't have friends, then."

"Not everybody is as tight-knit as you and your gang."

She scowled. "We're not a gang, and you shouldn't

be so quick to dismiss, as you're going to need us in the coming weeks."

Weeks? Devin fought a cold sweat. His vow not to get mixed up with Calla was shaky after they'd spent a few hours together. He'd never last weeks.

Or would he? Was he making too much out of their attraction? He'd been working virtually nonstop the past few weeks, closing several cases. He needed…companionship. Maybe if he gave into his urges, he'd get her out of his system. Then he could be in the same room with her without panting.

Although telling her that plan would buy him a one-way ticket out the door.

She waved her hand in front of his face. "Gone to la-la land already?"

No way. He'd be in a better mood if he had. "This whole thing will be cleared up in a few days. Neither the department nor IAB will take the word of a sole witness." Which was a good thing for him, since his record wasn't exactly spotless where the cops' cops were concerned. "They'll have to find physical evidence. They won't, since I didn't touch the guy."

"Evidence like the scrapes on your knuckles?"

He glanced down at his hands, noting the raw skin on his right. His heart jumped. "I hadn't noticed them."

"You're confused and probably have a splitting headache. It's understandable."

"No," he said slowly, "it really isn't. I'm a trained observer. Why didn't I see that?"

"The doctor said you'd have some side effects from the blow to your head. Shock and confusion are numbers one and two. Are you dizzy, as well? You should probably lie down awhile. We can table this discussion for now."

"I'm not dizzy," he ground out. He wasn't going to let her treat him like a scared kid. Or, worse, a victim.

The mistakes of the past were rounding on him with a vengeance. He already had a huge blemish on his record. The chances of his lieutenant standing by him over another one weren't good.

Infuriated and embarrassed, he turned to pace, wobbled on his feet and grasped the air for balance. She was on him in a second, sliding her arm around his waist. "I've got you."

Closing his eyes to her compassion, he longed to shoot something—preferably the creep who'd whacked him—but they'd taken his damn gun.

He didn't resist when she led him to the sofa, though he knew he should. Ever since he'd woken up, he'd felt as if time were jumping forward, then pausing, rewinding, then jerking ahead again. Yet of all the things he had no idea about, he knew one thing for certain: time moved in only one direction.

"I expect you'll remember everything eventually," Calla said, sitting beside him, wrapping her hand around his. "Though some people who're severely traumatized never fully regain—"

"I'm *not* traumatized."

"Whatever you say, Detective."

What happened to *Devin?* Last night she'd— There was the rewind again. He recalled sliding his hand between her thighs, his name on her lips as she…told him to back off.

Great. The idiotic behavior he'd sort-of remembered earlier hadn't been imaginary. He should really slink home before he humiliated himself further.

Her thumb glided across the back of his hand, and he went hard. Oh, good, to add to the complications he

had no idea how to solve, now his head wasn't the only part of him throbbing.

"Do you want to lie down or continue talking about suspects for your assault?" she asked.

"Suspects," he said quickly. Lying down meant a bed and sheets and— "I need to clear this up and get back to my life."

Her gaze flicked to his. Her blue eyes were bright and clear and so beautiful. He didn't belong in the same room with her, much less deserve her loyalty. "I kind of like having you here at my mercy."

"I don't like relying on anybody."

"No kidding." She glanced at their hands. "Not that I want you suspended, I just…" Snagging her tablet of notes from the coffee table, she sat on a bar stool across the room. "The guy who hit you is trying to frame you for assault, get you fired and arrested, sent to prison even. That's a pretty serious plan for a common street thief. Does anybody stand out among your cases?"

"I haven't arrested anybody who was happy about it."

"But in-the-moment fury is different than this. This is cold, hard rage. Somebody planned the attack on you." Her expression full of consideration, she propped her chin against her fist. "They planned it carefully, maybe for a long time. They turned your job against you."

The medication must have kicked in because Devin had no idea where she was going. "How so?"

"The thief-attacker-fake victim lured you to do your job then made you pay for it the way criminals pay. It's symbolic."

"Most convicts aren't deep thinkers. They look for a quick score. You're making too much drama out of this."

She dismissed the idea with a flick of her hand. "Probably. A writer's prerogative."

"You write travel articles, not mystery novels." Still, the idea of a plan to take him out couldn't be dismissed, since that's exactly what had happened. "So this guy pretends to be a purse snatcher and runs by me. How did he know I'd be in that bar at that time of day? How could he be sure I'd go after him?"

"He's watching you."

"Nobody tails me without me knowing about it."

"But you were distracted yesterday. Your day off, the neighbor's ceiling fan, the dry cleaning, football, the wedding. Regular guy stuff. You weren't in police mode."

"Cops, even off-duty ones, never stop being cops."

"If you say so."

He wished he could blame his countless mistakes yesterday on "regular guy stuff." In truth, the only thing that might have distracted him was the thought of seeing her, and he wasn't about to admit his weakness in that particular area.

Could he have been followed? He'd been running full-out over the past few days. Paperwork and court on Wednesday. Late stakeout on Thursday night. Arrest early Friday. But his schedule wasn't any more hectic this week than any other. He would have noticed some creep tailing him.

"So we start with career guys," she said, scribbling on her notepad. "Those with long memories and a score to settle."

"No." Devin rose. He was wobbly, which he hated, but he was still a cop. It was time he started acting like one. "We start with the scene of the crime."

CALLA WASN'T SURE how she wound up in a Midtown alley, peeking around a Dumpster, kicking her way around bits of trash and discarded food containers. The owner of the Chinese take-out joint they were lurking behind was destined to open his back door eventually, then they'd have some awkward explaining to do.

The fact that she and Devin found themselves on the opposite side of his coworkers was a development she'd never anticipated.

Since she'd known him, Devin had used his position to help people and serve the cause of justice. He found himself parted from the law now, and she honestly thought she and her friends might be his only hope. She was going to help him whether he wanted her to or not.

She owed him.

So regardless of what he wanted, she wasn't going to give up on him. Once he got his badge back, she'd decide if anything personal was worth pursuing.

Seriously, did the man always run from women who kissed him?

Not a reaction she'd expected from Detective Bad-ass, to say the least.

Said detective seemed to have forgotten she was there, though she found it hard to be insulted. He was no doubt reliving the assault from the night before.

She imagined him running into the alley, expecting to see the retreating back of his thief. Instead, he'd gotten clocked.

Had his cell phone flown free in the attack? Had he crawled toward it when he regained consciousness? Had he been afraid?

She looked toward him as he knelt on the pavement,

running his fingertips across the ground. "Anything?" she asked as she approached.

Not looking up, he shook his head. "I remember chasing him here, then…nothing."

"So he was the one who hit you?"

"No." Slowly, he straightened. "He was running away from me when I got hit."

"The accomplice, lying in wait. He clobbered you."

"We'd figured that already, but it's good to have confirmation." Laying his hand on the back of his head, he winced. "Though I swear I can feel the blow all over again."

"Meds haven't kicked in?"

"I see two of you, so I think they have." Though he turned away, she heard him mutter, "Not that double vision of you is a bad thing."

She ignored the compliment. Given their unsteady relationship, she thought she'd be wiser to focus on the assault. "And you never got a sense of anybody behind you? A movement? A shadow? A smell even?"

"Nothing."

"Do you remember what hit you? The guy didn't strike you with his bare hand. He had to be holding something."

"A bat, I guess."

She planted her hands on her hips. "Some guy wandered down Ninth Avenue with a bat, then darted into an alley and nobody questioned him?"

"It was dark and chilly," Devin said, narrowing his eyes. "Maybe the guy wore a coat."

"Did he?" she shot back.

"How should I—" He paused, cocking his head. "Maybe I passed somebody as I was walking."

"Did you?"

"I don't know," he returned, irritated. "I was... distracted."

"By?"

"You." He sighed. "I wanted to see you."

"Oh." Talk about lousy timing. What might have happened if he hadn't run into the thief's trap? Would they have spent the night together in an entirely different way?

"I need to go," he said. "I need some space."

She grabbed his arm as he moved past her. "You can't wander around the city alone. Let me take you home."

"Sure." He shook off her touch and stalked toward the end of the alley. "I'll hail a cab."

Watching him go, she noted the distance between them was greater than ever.

He blamed himself, not her, for not anticipating his attack. But if he didn't stow his temper, they were never going to get through this mess. He'd been there for her and her friends. Even when their actions had skirted the law, he'd stood by them.

As she followed him toward the street, she reminded herself of his guidance and support.

But damned if the man wasn't the most irritating, prickly, son of a—

Her tirade ground to a halt as she noticed a piece of gold fabric dangling from a shrub branch.

She brought the fabric to her nose and smelled a hint of gardenia, so it couldn't have been there long. What potential assaulter wore silken gold? None she could think of...unless an early Halloween sale at the costume shop two blocks over had brought out the animal side in a lame-seeking party girl.

The police had certainly searched the crime scene, so the chances of the fabric having anything to do with

Devin's case were less than zero. Still, she shoved the gold scrap into the front pocket of her jeans. Maybe she could find a way to have it professionally examined.

When she reached the end of the alley, a cab was waiting along with Devin, his hand outstretched. "How about if I buy lunch?" he suggested as he assisted her into the car.

He kept hold of her hand as he directed the cab to a deli several blocks away, and less than twenty minutes later, Calla found herself at his kitchen table, enjoying a gooey, piping hot slice of pepperoni-and-sausage pizza.

His third-floor apartment, with a lovely view of the tree-lined street below, was large, though additions were spare. Plain furniture, probably rented, a couple of standard landscapes on the walls and no photographs or mementos. A couple of gun magazines had been tossed on the coffee table, and a book on forensics lay open and facedown on the sofa. The living room and kitchen walls were painted dove-gray, the bedroom—which she'd gotten a peek of from the hallway—was a dark, grayish-blue. Like a storm in the summer sky.

The colors suited him, and she'd bet her next assignment to any tropical paradise that everything that actually belonged to him could fit into a suitcase and two boxes.

"I'm sorry about before," he said as he pushed away his empty plate and leaned back in his chair. "None of this is your fault."

"Nor yours."

He said nothing.

"I'm willing to make allowances for your mood," she added. "Considering the circumstances." Hiding a smile, she sipped her soda. "You're not the cheeriest guy when you aren't accused of assault."

"And you're full of sweetness and light."

She wagged her finger at him. "Stow the sarcasm, Detective. I'm on your side, remember?"

"I wasn't being sarcastic. I was completely serious."

"Ah, so I'm sugary and you're dark and brooding."

"Yes."

As silly as the idea seemed, she had a feeling this difference was the reason he was keeping his distance from her. "Do you always run from sweet women who kiss you?"

He rose to clear the table. "Sweet women don't kiss me."

"So I'm a...special case."

He paused, loading the dishwasher before answering. "Yes."

She followed him into the kitchen. "I made the first move. Somebody had to."

"I'm not so sure. We need time apart."

"Why?"

"Since I don't—" He stopped, shoving the dishwasher door closed. "I'd like your help. There's nobody else. But I can't get into anything with anybody right now. I need to get my badge back. I *have* to."

Though she didn't like the idea that she was *anybody,* Calla walked toward him. "You have my loyalty, Detective. Always."

"Thanks. You can call me by my first name, you know."

"Why would I do that?"

"Like you said, we're friends."

She crossed her arms over her chest. "Are we?"

"I thought so. Last night..."

"How much of last night do you remember?"

"Bits and pieces." His gaze connected with hers,

then slid away. "I made a move, you rejected. Smart decision."

"You were pretty out of it. I didn't want repercussions later. I wondered if you might blame your attraction to me on booze and a concussion."

"You think I'm attracted to you?"

"Yes." And she was becoming more confident by the second. He didn't want to want her, but he did. "And there's nobody else, right?"

"I've had plenty of lovers. Right now I need a friend."

He was, very politely and firmly, putting their desire for each other aside. Given all he'd gone through in the past day, she'd let him get away with avoidance.

For the moment.

"You have not just one, but three friends." She paused, reconsidering. "Five, if you count the guys."

Sighing, he crossed his arms over his chest. "Please make it clear to your gang that they're not allowed to burgle, interrogate or unlawfully enter a residence or place of business."

She opened her mouth to argue, since—who was he kidding?—she and her friends would likely break all those rules in the first forty-eight hours if they needed to, but he rolled on before she could point out the obvious.

"I'm in charge of this case. And while the NYPD and I might be at odds, I'm the one with the badge, so you girls will follow my orders." He opened the pantry door and knelt, rummaging around the floor as she glared at his back. "Surveillance would be good. I'll put you on watching the purse snatcher."

"As soon as you find out who he is," she returned smartly.

He either didn't hear or didn't care about her sarcasm. "And try not to be too obvious. Wear a hat."

"A hat?" she repeated.

"Yeah. You glow like the noonday sun."

"I glow?" she asked, now treading the line between aggravation and flattery. Did the man live to keep her off balance?

When he stood and turned toward her, he was holding a pistol.

Yep, apparently he did.

As much as she liked looking at him, she couldn't seem to move her gaze from the gun. "Where did that come from?"

"My safe." He shoved an ammunition clip into the butt of the pistol. "Beretta nine-millimeter. I like a classic."

"So I see. What're you doing with it?"

He shrugged on a leather shoulder holster and slid the gun into the slot below his left arm. "Like you said, somebody's after me. I need to take precautions."

"But you're not allowed to…" She trailed off at the fierce look that flooded his face. Clearing her throat, she made herself continue. She wasn't afraid of guns. She was a Texan. But she was wildly concerned about what Devin might do with his weapon. "You can't carry a gun in the city."

"I'm not walking around unarmed."

"You have to."

"Weapons laws aren't my problem."

Calla had a feeling they would be very soon.

And he was worried about her randomly interrogating people.

"Okay," she said, backing away while mentally making a note to check if bail could be posted for some-

body with a credit card; otherwise, she'd have to run by an ATM. "Let's get to work on your recent cases. Anybody who outright threatened you should be noted. We'll fill in the details once we get more information from the department."

"And how exactly are we going to get anything out of them?"

"We'll ask."

5

DEVIN WASN'T SURE HOW she'd done it, but over the next several days Calla had gotten access to closed case files and made copies of all the ones he'd mentioned as possibles for revenge against him. He was grateful and impressed.

At least until she'd turned his apartment into a chick club.

They'd shared wedding pictures, cookie recipes, clothes and shoes, profit margins for their various businesses, city gossip, restaurant health ratings, how men were so cute but dense, the economy, how that was impacting their various businesses.

Devin's head had starting spinning after the first ten minutes. He'd take a shoot-out in a dark alley any day. He'd stopped taking pain pills days ago, but he was tempted to head to the medicine cabinet.

Instead, he crossed to the fridge for a beer.

"It's barely four o'clock," Calla said in reproach.

He made a show of twisting off the top of a bottle. "I'm not on duty."

"Which is stupid," Victoria commented. "Aren't my

tax dollars paying your salary? We need good cops on the streets."

"And we're certainly less one with Devin on suspension," Shelby said.

Flicking her dark hair off her face, Victoria scowled, her icy-blue eyes fierce. "Idiotic bureaucracy. I say screw 'em. There's got to be a law firm in this city that needs a solid investigator."

"I don't know about that," Calla said, shaking her head as she scooped cookie dough onto a baking sheet. "What if he winds up following around potential divorcees, trying to prove adultery or other nasty habits?"

"He'd be terrific as a subpoena server," Shelby pointed out. "All that dark energy and quiet stares."

"You three know I'm standing right here, don't you?" Devin asked. He snagged a warm cookie off the cooling rack. "And I already have a job." Though the meal perks of being suspended were a nice reward for his troubles.

Victoria drummed her fingers against the kitchen table. "Pretty lousy of your employers to spend their time investigating you when they should be looking at that sketchy thief and this obvious framing."

"They have to follow procedure," Devin said—for probably the tenth time.

The Take Matters Into Your Own Hands Gang obviously didn't know the meaning of legal protocol.

But he could hardly argue with their techniques. They got results, and that was what he needed. Ethics and consequences were on indefinite hold.

Though he hadn't said so, he understood their drive to circumvent the rules better than most. As a kid growing up in an abusive household, he'd been bitter about teachers and social workers who hadn't seen what was really going on and saved him from his personal hell.

But once he'd earned his badge, he'd accepted the rules that went along with it. He promised himself he'd make a difference, and he'd do it the right way. He wasn't sure what it said about him that, though he'd previously adopted an aberrance for vigilantism, he was not just willing, but eager, to compromise when it was his ass on the line.

"Phooey on procedure," Calla said, making a classic get lost gesture.

A smokin' hot blond Texan who knew how to tell somebody to piss off without a word? Was it any wonder he was crazy about her?

He had to admit his surprise that for all Calla's sweet requests and enticing wiles, she still hadn't gotten the identity of the thief out of his lieutenant. Even the peanut butter chocolate chunk cookies and Calla in a miniskirt had failed.

Being faced with such temptation himself, Devin had to admire Meyer's resistance.

Seeing her, inhaling her and enjoying her smiles for the past few days had weakened his resolve for keeping his distance to the point that he was seriously considering the idea of giving in. Just once. Surely if they exorcised their attraction, they'd get past the carnal need and be able to go back to casual friends.

Beyond that torturous indecision, he was also in limbo with his suspension. He expected IAB every day, but was confused why they hadn't yet questioned him. The delay had him antsy. Something big was going on, and he hoped he wasn't the prize pig destined for a long, slow roast.

He refused to ask his buddies in the department for help. One, it was humiliating. Two, he didn't want them tossing in their chips on a bad hand.

Just how thorough was the frame-up?

Devin grabbed another cookie, though the smell of a chicken-and-cheese casserole Shelby had made permeated the apartment. Once this mess was over, he'd be back to burgers and wings at the pub, so he might as well enjoy the unexpected gifts.

Shelby, her expression stern, rushed toward him with a mixing bowl tucked under her arm. "Dinner's in less than an hour."

Devin shoved the rest of the cookie in his mouth. "I'll eat that, too."

"Bottomless pit," she muttered, a hint of cinnamon and sugar trailing after her.

Devin followed her. "Don't worry, my lovely harem," he said, spreading his arms. "I won't lose my appetite."

The three women stared at him.

He surveyed the beautiful group gathered at his slightly battered kitchen table—the blonde, the brunette and the redhead. If he was a bragging kind of guy, he'd take a picture and post his coop online. Though, since he wasn't sure how long he'd have a job or a reputation, he didn't have much of an urge to whip out his phone and start clicking.

"Devin," Calla began, her fingertip tapping a stack of suspect files, "we're trying to work. You could help by deciphering these notes you made. Your handwriting is terrible."

And the fantasy comes to a crashing halt....

"Seriously, Antonio...harem?" Victoria snorted with mock laughter. "In your dreams, copper."

He certainly had plenty of those. But they all involved one woman.

When he moved toward her to help with the handwriting problem, a whiff of her vanilla-scented lotion

washed over him, and he squeezed his eyes shut to gather his resistance.

"Are you in pain, Detective?" he heard Shelby asked, concerned.

He opened his eyes. "No." At least not the kind of pain she was wondering about.

"You're not fully recovered from your injury." Shelby pulled out a kitchen chair. "Sit. Didn't the doctor say you could have headaches and dizzy spells for weeks?"

"I'm fine," he snapped, caught between embarrassment and arousal.

Hurt flicked across her face, and he regretted his attitude. He'd never been mothered before. He wasn't exactly sure how to act.

"Thank you," he added in a softer tone. "I think better on my feet." He turned his attention to the folder Calla was holding. "GSW," he said, looking at the list over her shoulder. "Gun shot wound."

"Oh." Calla paused then, asked, "You'd think a guy who stole a snake would have been bitten, not shot."

Damn, she was cute. "A Viper's a sports car, not a serpent."

"Oh." She paused for a longer stretch this time. "Why would you want to ride in something named after a poisonous—" Abruptly, she waved her hand. "Never mind."

"This isn't the guy I chased," Devin said. "Look at his weight—two-sixty. The handbag thief was short, wiry and fast. He outpaced me for more than a block."

Victoria handed Calla another folder. "Let's talk about this one."

Devin studied the information, and his cop sensors went on alert. This guy was destined for a long career. He'd been picked up as a kid on minor theft and van-

dalism, graduated to assault and armed robbery in his early twenties. Hard, having suffered serious abuse in childhood, he'd resisted all efforts at education and rehabilitation.

He'd been released from prison two weeks ago.

"Scary-lookin' dude," Calla commented.

"And no dummy, either," Devin said, remembering the guy well. "He'd ripped off five convenience stores in Midtown before we got him. And we only managed that because some tourist happened to get a cell phone video of him running from the scene."

"He was locked up six years, though," Shelby pointed out. "You think he'd really come for you after all those years?"

Victoria spoke before Devin could decide. "Nothing much to do in prison but eat, sleep and plot what you're going to do when you get out."

They all agreed on the sageness of that fact.

Looking at several other files, they found more possibilities, but Devin couldn't help but think they were simply marking time until IAB rapped on his door. "This is great, ladies, but when Internal Affairs questions me, they'll tell me the identity of my accuser."

Maybe when he had that information, and he could pair it with the cases they'd been researching, he'd find a link.

But then he'd also have to endure another encounter with IAB. The last one hadn't been pretty.

Calla narrowed her eyes. "You mean the thief."

Devin nodded. "Seems like there's more evidence against me than him, though. If I'm gonna be charged, they'll tell me that, too."

Victoria's head snapped up. "What charges exactly?"

Devin shrugged with a casualness he certainly didn't feel. "Assault."

"You're a cop," Shelby said. "Aren't you allowed to hit bad guys?"

"Only if they swing first."

"But you were assaulted, too," Calla said.

"They'll think I hit myself to cover up my assault of a suspect."

Victoria rolled her eyes. "Oh, please."

Before Devin could do more than marvel at the loyalty from his defense team, his phone buzzed. Pulling it from his back pocket, he noted the text from a buddy at the department. *Be ready. IAB coming today.*

After relaying the information, the mood in the apartment dived. Dinner's tempting smell could still be detected, but there was no denying the concern.

When the knock came, Devin headed to the door without looking at Calla or the others. Part of him wished they weren't there, part of him knew he couldn't deal with this mess alone, much as that was his natural instinct.

A guy in a tailored navy suit stood in the hall. He held up his NYPD badge. "Lieutenant Colin Reid, Internal Affairs."

"Yeah." Devin stepped back and allowed the other man to enter. "I've seen you around."

His short brown hair looked as if the edges had been measured with a ruler, then trimmed with a razor blade. Devin had the feeling he and this guy weren't going to be buds.

When he and Reid entered the living room-kitchen area, the case files were miraculously gone, and the ladies looked busy doing anything but conducting their version of a private investigation. Shelby and Victoria

hovered near the stove, while Calla appeared thoroughly engrossed in *Guns and Ammo.*

How much of this Reid bought, Devin couldn't tell. The lieutenant's face was blank as he surveyed the apartment. "I need a word in private, Detective."

All pretense at reading the magazine abandoned, Calla surged to her feet. "I'd like to stay."

"You're entitled to a lawyer," Reid said.

Devin scowled. "Do I need one?"

Reid shrugged. "Legal representation is generally more advisable than a friend."

Devin didn't hesitate. "Calla can stay."

Silently, Reid stared at the other two women.

Shelby tugged Victoria's arm. "We need to go to the bakery and get bread for dinner."

"Can't you *make* bread?" Victoria asked incredulously as the two retreated down the hall.

"I expected you days ago," Devin said to Reid when the door closed behind them.

Reid removed a micro-recorder from his briefcase. "We had priority cases to clear."

"Do you people ever give a straight answer?" Calla asked, irritated.

By the surprise that skated across Reid's face, Devin knew he, like so many others before him, had underestimated the angelic-looking blonde.

"I'll be asking the questions today," Reid said, recovering quickly.

Devin and Calla sat side by side on the sofa, while Reid sat in a chair across from them once he'd set the recorder on the coffee table.

He started the interview by reciting the standard warnings regarding statements and legal representation.

He asked Devin a few opening questions about his

position with the department and years of service. Reid certainly knew the answers already but was watching Devin's body language closely. If his mannerisms or tone of voice changed, it could signal a lie.

The fact that Devin understood Reid's strategy didn't give him any comfort, however.

He then went through the events of Saturday night, and Devin was glad Calla had encouraged him to write down his account. The chain of events came easily to mind, and he could recite the account with confidence.

Cops noticed details and telling IAB he couldn't remember because of the lump on his head would be tantamount to an admission of guilt at worst, or he was incompetent at his job at best.

"How much did you drink before you saw the alleged thief?" Reid asked.

Devin clenched his teeth at the underlying insult. "One beer. Off duty," he couldn't help but add.

"And you saw nobody in the alley other than the alleged thief?"

Devin had already said he hadn't but he answered calmly, "No."

"How quickly after entering the alley were you allegedly struck?"

Call surged to her feet. "*Allegedly?* Would you like to see the baseball-size knot on his head? What kind of cop are you, questioning a fellow officer instead of the criminal he was chasing?"

Devin grabbed her hand and pulled her to the sofa. "Calla, please."

"Where are you from?" Reid asked, his gaze locked on Calla.

Devin resisted the urge to smile. He'd asked her the same question in the same baffled tone not too long ago.

"Texas," Calla returned. "We take justice very seriously."

"Nice to know." Reid didn't acknowledge Calla's outburst further, he simply continued interrogating in the same monotone.

He went over Devin's statement backward and forward. He jumped around the time frame and asked the same question more than once—all in an effort to shake Devin's confidence.

The tactic didn't work.

Despite sensing Calla's simmering fury beside him, Devin kept his gaze on Reid's face. He knew he'd accomplished his own goal when frustration jumped into Reid's muddy-brown eyes.

It was easily the most entertaining moment in the past five days.

When he'd run out of redundant questions, Reid stood and returned the recorder to his briefcase. "Thank you for your time, Detective. I'll be in touch."

"The name, Reid," Devin said before he could turn away. "Who's the guy?"

After a slight pause, Reid answered. "Jimmie Forrester."

Devin's brain provided an image of a wiry, twitchy, well-known thief. "Jimmie Forrester says I hit him in an alley," he said in disbelief.

Reid nodded.

"Jumpin' Jimmie—the same guy I arrested two years ago for burglary?"

Interest flicked across Reid's features. "So you remember him."

"I remember I outweigh him by forty pounds, and his head barely reaches my shoulder. He couldn't lift a bat to hit me with." But the description fit the guy he'd

chased. The thief had been wearing a ball cap and overcoat, so it could've been Jumpin' Jimmie. "He also got a six-month sentence in a mental health facility because he supposedly has a compulsion to steal."

"Nobody said he was wise to pick a fight with you, and he has a documented psychiatric condition."

"Bull." Devin paced. "This whole business stinks. I know it. You know it."

Reid shrugged. "I have an incident to investigate."

"It wasn't only me and Jimmie in that alley. Investigate that."

"I'll be thorough," Reid promised. "Particularly as your record has a distinctive blemish already."

Devin stilled. He didn't dare glance at Calla. He might have known IAB would bring up the past, but he still felt the punch to his gut. "As thorough as you are, I doubt anybody's file is unmarked."

Reid might have been an uptight prig, but he must have sensed he'd gone too far. Whether he didn't want to piss off Devin further or embarrass him in front of Calla, the lieutenant nodded. "Cops should be above reproach."

Calla glared at him. "I'm so glad everything is neat and tidy in your little world."

Reid headed down the hall. "Unfortunately, it's not. But somebody has to man the broom."

6

WHEN SHE FINALLY unclenched her fist, Calla was sure her nails had drawn blood from her palm.

To witness Devin being forced to answer humiliating questions was almost more than she could stand. She almost wished she'd left with her friends, but feared abandoning him would have been a worse choice.

And yet her conscience couldn't forget the stony lieutenant's accusation. *Particularly as your record has a distinctive blemish already.*

The suspension from three years before. She'd known about it for months. Obviously it was time to find out the cause.

"What record?" she asked Devin pointedly when the door closed behind Reid.

"That was fun," he said, stalking toward the kitchen.

She charged after him. "Does he mean the suspension from before? What happened three years ago?"

From the refrigerator shelf, Devin yanked out the beer he'd started on before Reid arrived. Defiantly, he took a sip. "You want a day-by-day account or merely the highlights?"

She scowled. "You're dodging."

He shrugged.

She stepped in front of him so quickly their bodies bumped. He jumped back as if he'd struck a tree. The only time she seemed able to throw him off stride was by physical contact. "My questions are important."

"Is dinner going to be ready anytime soon? I think better on a full stomach."

"No, you don't. You're either running full out or napping on the sofa. I need a gear somewhere in between that allows me to find out what blemish is on your record."

He dropped the facade of politeness. "My record. My business."

Oh, he had to be kidding. But she was used to his reticence by now, so instead of leading with her simmering temper, she laid her hand on his chest. She'd let him set aside their desire, but alone with him, tensions high, the lion roared back to life. "Still trying to keep your distance?"

"I'm trying to save my career."

"I'm trying to help you."

"Why?" His hard gaze was unavoidable as he asked the question. "Why do you care?"

Was she letting her needs rule her senses? Had she placed her faith in a corrupt cop? Was it blind belief on her part?

She'd actually witnessed him bending the rules. He'd done so for her and her friends. At their request. Had he done the same for others?

"I owe you," she said finally, not going anywhere near their unresolved romantic emotions. The ones where he sent her longing messages, the ones where he held her close and looked at her with the heat and hunger she'd only glimpsed, the ones in which they

finally satisfied the ache they'd managed to bury so deeply for so long.

He glanced at her hand against his body but otherwise didn't move. "You don't."

"You've appreciated my help so far." She paused, realizing by the remote look in his eyes that they'd reached a crossroads. "As long as I don't get too close."

"Exactly."

"And I'm getting too close?"

He stepped back, not only physically, but in every way. Whatever secrets he had, he wasn't going to share with her. "Yes."

"Why won't you let me inside?"

"There's nothing to see. Nothing worth knowing."

Drained of her fight and her will, Calla turned from him. "Maybe you're right." All she wanted to do now was escape. "Enjoy your dinner. And your solitude."

"I COULD TAKE THE BREAD by," Shelby whispered, pointing at the bag of French-style loaves she'd shoved under the table. "Make sure he's okay."

Unable to forget the distant expression in Devin's eyes, Calla pushed her fork through her untouched pasta in pesto sauce. "Whatever."

"Forget Antonio," Victoria said. "We need glasses and pink spray paint."

Shelby frowned. "What the devil for?"

Victoria patted Calla's hand. "I think poor Pollyanna's broken."

"That's not funny." Calla made an effort to sit straight. "I'm fine."

"Sweetie," Shelby began after a quick glance at Victoria, "you're many wonderful things, but fine isn't one of them."

After leaving Devin's apartment, Calla had texted her friends to meet her at a neighborhood restaurant. If he wanted to do everything on his own, he damn well could have at it.

But her desire for him lingered, and her guilt at leaving him when he needed her the most—even though he refused to admit it—was growing.

"He needs a lawyer," Calla said, not wanting to admit how much she was dwelling on Devin's rejection.

Victoria's mouth tightened before she worked up a smile. "That I can do."

Shelby angled her head in confusion. "I thought we decided one of your dad's buddies would be too expensive."

Victoria waved her hand. "They are. I was talking about Howard."

"We're not dragging Howard into this," Calla said firmly.

"He's willing," Victoria argued. "Which is more than we can say for Antonio. What more do you want?"

"Somebody else," Calla returned. "Anybody else."

"I'm siding with Calla on this," Shelby said, earning her a frustrated frown from Victoria. "Howard would be intimidated by Antonio. Probably not the best start to an attorney-client relationship."

"I can't imagine anybody having a smooth ride with Antonio," Victoria said, jabbing at her Caesar salad with her fork.

Shelby paused in reaching for the pepper grinder. "She's not wrong there."

"I was actually thinking more about Howard's feelings," Calla clarified. "It took a while to let him down gently. I don't like the idea of reigniting his crush."

Victoria scooped up a bite of salad. "Ah, Pollyanna lives again."

Crossing her arms over her chest, Calla leaned back in her chair. "I could use a little support here."

"I've been supportive," Victoria said, her eyes glinting with fierceness. "I've listened and advised. I even cooked. But I think it's time we all get real."

"V, do you think now—"

Victoria silenced Shelby with a single lift of her finger. "Antonio is a good cop. He's been there for us several times over the last six months. But he doesn't want our help."

Shelby leaned in. "I'm not sure about that. He wants it, but doesn't know how to accept it."

Victoria's pale blue eyes, still focused on Calla, narrowed. "Then too damn bad for him. He's a grown man and ought to know what he wants and doesn't. We're feeding him, consoling him and considering what lawyer to hire, while he's avoiding questions and keeping secrets." Victoria shook her head. "That isn't going to work."

Calla dropped her gaze to her plate. She couldn't face her friends—or the truth about Devin. "I like him," she whispered reluctantly.

Her friends' hands immediately covered hers. "We kinda figured that," Shelby said.

Calla clenched her fists. "You guys think he's *Calla-dazzled*, remember? Why won't he let me in?"

"Some men don't know how," Shelby said gently.

"A lot of men can't," Victoria added.

"You have men who do." A quick glance at her friends and their identical winces made her want to recall her comment. "I'm not jealous," she added in a rush. "I have a full life, I just…"

She trailed off, not knowing what she wanted.

With little choice, she waved off the personal stuff. "What in the world could he have done to get suspended the first time?"

"He probably insulted somebody important," Shelby offered.

"Or ate too many doughnuts," Victoria said.

"Not with a body like that," Calla muttered.

Victoria smiled—well, victoriously. "Oh, yeah? What do you know about his body?"

"I had to undress him before I put him in my bed the other night. He smelled like whiskey and cigarette smoke. Which defies explanation, by the way. What bar in the city lets you smoke these days? You can't even smoke outside in the parks. Regardless, I had to get those clothes in the washer. I'd never get that horrible smell out of my Egyptian cotton sheets."

"Talk about burying the lead," Shelby said, her eyes wide.

"I'm a feature writer, not a reporter," Calla returned with a smirk.

Victoria tapped her fingertip on the table. "How did you manage to leave out the naked part of your grand rescue?"

Calla cleared her throat and tried, without much success, to banish the glorious vision of Devin's leanly muscled body from her memory. "I focused on the immediate problem instead of extraneous details."

"Extraneous?" Victoria repeated incredulously. "The lack of nakedness between the two of you is the reason we're all here wallowing in—"

"Hang on," Shelby jumped in. "So when Antonio woke up Sunday morning, in your bed, he was naked?"

Calla hesitated before she admitted, "Well, yeah."

"Certainly explains why he was confused about whether or not you two had had sex." Shelby pursed her lips. "You didn't have sex, right?"

"No, of course not," Calla said. "We're supposed to be talking about Devin's record."

"I'd say he's zero for one." Victoria poured more wine into her glass. "Wouldn't you?"

"V, please," Shelby admonished.

In consolation, Victoria added wine into the other two glasses. "Just reminding you both of where we stand. What man wouldn't want our brilliant, buxom Calla? The dude is either gay, crazy or carrying serious baggage."

"But he's a good cop," Calla reminded her. "You said so a few minutes ago."

"I think he gets the job done at all cost," Victoria responded.

"An attitude that leads to either justice or trouble," Shelby pointed out. "In his case, that could easily translate to a professional splotch or two." Shelby met Calla's gaze. "Everybody has regrets."

Everything her friends said was true. Why was Calla hanging on to the dream that Devin would one day notice her and be grateful she was by his side? Why was she hurt and surprised he wouldn't tell her about his past?

He'd certainly never claimed or pretended to be Mr. Sunshine, but she *was* Pollyanna.

HUDDLED ON THE SOFA with a cup of tea gone cold, a fleece blanket and a weepy romance DVD, Calla blinked dazedly at the knocking sound at her apartment door.

Anger, frustration, wine and most of her dinner in

a take-out box wasn't the combination for a peaceful night apparently.

Grumbling under her breath, she tossed aside the blanket and stumbled to the door. If this was her neighbor, ancient Mrs. Winsley, who thought somebody was breaking into her apartment every other minute, she was going to forget she was a nice person.

She flung open the door, prepared to blast whoever dared stand on the other side and invade her nightmare.

It was Devin.

A fluffy beige cat was tucked in the crooked of his arm. At her appearance, the cat blinked its big green eyes and meowed with great annoyance.

Her heart melted. Though the cat's coloring was a combo of her and Devin, it obviously had his personality. Good grief.

Dragging her gaze from the cat, she met the identical green of Devin's eyes. She steeled herself against the urge to get lost in the regret reflected back at her. "I'm surprised you remember where I live."

"I'm a cop. Well, sort of. I can still investigate."

"And Fluffy?" When he looked baffled, she pointed at the cat. "I don't remember you having a pet."

"An adoption notice went out on the NYPD email loop. His owner was killed in a hit and run. I thought you two might get along."

A hit and run. There was no end to the man's romantic streak.

"Do you take bribes?" she asked on a sigh instead of in a temper. The cat was incredibly cute, after all.

"No."

She opened the door wider and moved aside so Devin could enter. "Lucky for you, I do."

"Fluffy?" he questioned as they headed toward the

living room. "I was thinking something cooler like Sharky."

Calla considered the ball of fluff with the killer eyes. "Sharky it is." When she reached the kitchen, she opened the fridge door. "I don't know what to feed a traumatized cat."

Devin held up a black plastic container, the kind the restaurants used for delivery. "I brought this."

Inside was leftover chicken casserole. She supposed it had been a lot for one person. Of course, if he hadn't been so difficult, he could have had three others join him for dinner.

Shaking aside the critical thought, she dished out a healthy spoonful on a saucer and put it on the kitchen floor. After Devin set the cat down, Sharky pounced as if he hadn't eaten in a month.

Calla studied him to delay the inevitable confrontation with Devin. "If he keeps that up, he'll be the size of tiger."

"He's been staying with Sergeant Franklin the last few days, and his diet is mostly street cart tacos and diet soda."

"A gourmet cat?"

"He'll fit right in with this gang. He can be the mascot. Do you want to keep him?"

You or him? Calla almost asked. Foolish. Hadn't she decided she was done being an idiot over him?

Kneeling, Calla stroked the cat's silky fur. Her purred beneath her touch. So easy, so right. She was hooked for sure now.

"I'm sorry."

She glanced up, more at the tender note in his voice than the actual words.

Before she could respond, he knelt beside her. "Hard

as it is to believe, I do understand friendship and compassion. You've been nothing but kind to me, and I've
been an ass. I'd like another chance." He tucked a loose
strand of her hair behind her ear. "I really do need you."

Unexpected, embarrassing tears clogged her throat.
How many times had she hoped to see that earnest look
in his eyes? She tried not to read too much into his need.
Or let her hope rule her head. He'd said friendship, not
undying love. "Okay," she managed to say.

He stood, dragging his hand through his hair. "And
I'd appreciate your advice on how to handle the information about Jimmie Forrester. I need more background
on him. You're the best researcher I know. Plus, I still
don't have a clue what happened the other night. Jimmie didn't hit me, and I sure as hell didn't hit him, so
who did? And why?"

Rising, she shrugged. Despite his apology and adorable gift, she was reluctant to jump back into her role
as assistant investigator.

"You're usually the wordy one. Say something."

"You're going to tell me about your record, right?
The reason behind your suspension?"

Looking only half as reluctant as she expected, he
nodded.

"An accomplice hit you both," she said easily, as that
seemed obvious to her.

"Accomplice to what? A purse snatching? That isn't
a two-man job. Even if it was, why would Jimmie's own
partner beat him up?"

"Maybe he agreed, so you could be framed for the
assault. Maybe the partner double-crossed him, and
you were a convenient fall guy for everything." She
angled her head as she considered. "There could have
been something extraordinarily valuable in the purse."

"Like money or jewelry?"

"Or a top secret microchip. The thieves could be spies."

"*Jimmie?* No way. He's small-time, and he doesn't have the brains for spying or the frame-up of a cop."

"Then we'll have to find out who does." She scooped up the cat, who'd finished eating and was staring at them and looking annoyed again. "I'll set up his litter box in the bathroom, you put on the coffee. Before we go forward, I'm gonna need a short history lesson."

"THREE YEARS AGO I WAS working with Homicide on a murder case," Devin began, leaning heavily on the balcony's iron railing.

He and Calla had moved outside—a risk in itself, as the patio was barely large enough for two people to stand on without touching toes. But the night was unexpectedly warm, and he could use the air and space to tell her about the painful past he never seemed able to put behind him.

"A guy had been stabbed in a conference room at the Marriott Marquis. A business exec in town for an accounting conference found him when she arrived to set up for her presentation. She ran screaming through the hotel. At least twenty accountants trampled the crime scene before a security guard was found. Blood tracked everywhere. Hysterical tourists. It was a big, damn mess.

"By the time our techs examined all the prints, blood splatter and other evidence, there was nothing to link the dead guy to his killer."

"Smart bad guy. Leave the body in a busy place where it would be discovered unexpectedly. Escape in a crowd of convention goers, random tourists and hotel

guests." She made a swirling motion with her hands. "Confusion ensues."

He glanced at her in surprise. Though she looked like The Sunshine Fairy, her thought process was seasoned investigator. He hadn't noticed the contrast until a few days ago when she'd made such meticulous notes about his assault. "But it's also risky," he said, wondering how she'd counter his challenge. "What if the body's found by security or somebody who doesn't panic?" As he recalled the chaotic crime scene, he added, "Anybody with sense."

"A tourist with sense?" she asked, rolling her eyes as she smiled. "What are the odds?"

That smile was her silver bullet. Or, in this gang's case, the golden arrow. Under her influence, thousands would confess and be led to jail without protest. Maybe he should throw himself on the mercy of the court and/or his scheming frame-up guys with her as his defense.

He really did need her—and in more than the obvious ways. Had he been so distracted by their attraction that he hadn't noticed everything else she was? Was he so afraid of tainting her with his dark life that he hadn't recognized her strength?

"Tourists can be smart," he conceded. "Definitely brighter than me, but not about a bloody stab wound."

"Exactly. So you're down to hoping the body's discovered by docs, cops, nurses and paramedics. Smart bad guy," she repeated.

"Or at least one who was willing to risk playing the panic odds." There was a strange parallel, actually, between the confusion of the night he'd chased the thief and the case that had changed the way he'd investigated. Though the similarity might simply be because he'd

been suspended as a result both times. Or that a stunning blonde had been on hand both times.

"She was," Devin said, his gaze drawn by the moon hanging brightly in the sky, outshining even Manhattan's brightest.

"Hang on. The killer was a woman?"

"The day after the murder, she found me at one of my pub haunts, claiming to be a cousin of the victim. She was beautiful, upset and lonely. I—"

"Made her less lonely," Calla finished before he could admit the nasty truth.

Devin clenched his jaw. Admitting his mistake in judgment wasn't nearly as difficult as telling Calla he'd lost his head over another woman. "I thought she was a concerned friend. She was his smuggling partner."

"And honor among thieves only goes so far."

"Apparently. We got her, thanks to determined work by my lieutenant and the rest of the team, though obviously not before my superiors uncovered our personal connection."

"Resulting in the suspension." She paused. "And a transfer out of Homicide."

"I was lucky I didn't lose my badge."

"Was this Lieutenant Meyer, by any chance?"

"No. He was the only one willing to take me on after the stabbing case." Devin closed his eyes against the image of Meyer being interrogating by straitlaced Colin Reid. "I owe him."

Calla pressed her lips to his cheek. "Things will be different this time."

His skin warmed by both her gesture and her touch. "How?"

"You've got me. And my friends." She glanced at the

kitten, curled up on a blanket at her feet. "Sharky, too. All great teams need a kick-ass mascot."

Since their fierce symbol was currently flopped on his back and sleeping off his chicken casserole, Devin wasn't sure of his advantage. But the cat had gotten him through Calla's door and back into her good graces— for now, anyway—so he had a permanent spot in the gang as far as Devin was concerned.

As he raised his gaze to Calla's face, he noticed what she was wearing, a filmy, pale yellow print dress. Her hair was piled on top of her head, and her lips were painted the same glossy pink as her toenails. His mouth went dry. Had he been so intent on his issues that he'd failed to notice his greatest asset was an angel?

"You're wearing a dress," he said like an idiot.

"Thanks for noticing," she returned without missing a beat.

"You were wrapped in a robe when I got here."

"And then I changed."

"Why?"

"I like to look nice. I usually wear this dress with these cute brown cowboy boots that I got on sale at Barney's."

How they'd gone from murder to shoe sales at a high-end department store was just one of the mysteries of their relationship. A relationship it might be time to stop fighting. Distance and his clumsy effort to be noble were getting him nowhere. "You're tougher than I thought you were," he said, for once letting himself delight in her adorable girliness.

"Tougher, how?" she asked suspiciously.

"Stronger, harder, resilient. Not so…"

"Pollyanna?"

Based on the scowl marring her beautiful lips, he decided not to agree with that assessment. "Fairylike."

"Have you been talking to Shelby and Victoria? Is this a Robin Hood thing?"

They weren't stealing anything, they weren't righting a wrong against the repressed and innocent, since he wasn't either. "I don't see how. Though, I guess he is a fairy tale."

"Not in my world." She turned her face toward the moon, leaving him with her stunning profile. "His ideology is as real as the Crusades themselves. We're going to make things right. You're going to get your badge back."

"I have no idea why, but I believe you."

"It's the Pollyanna Plague." She took a step toward him. Given the size of the balcony, they bumped chests. "Very contagious."

At her proximity, his heart picked up speed. "I appreciate everything you and your friends are doing. But untangling this plot of a known thief, his assault and the reasons for it all is gonna be the biggest challenge…well, since the last time I was suspended. And since that will require all my effort, I've been thinking that the tension between us gets in the way of concentrating on work."

At the end of his rambling, she blinked. "You're into long speeches these days." Her gaze dropped to his lips. "What tension exactly?"

"The I-want-you kind."

"Which you're admitting all of a sudden."

"Seems stupid to continue to deny it."

"How sensible of you. How do you propose we get rid of it?"

"Sleep with me."

She coughed. "Boy, when you decide to solve a problem, you dive right in."

"I'm not good at subterfuge." He slipped his arms around her waist. "Pretending the attraction isn't there hasn't worked so far. I figure if we get the sex out of the way, we can be more relaxed around each other."

"Gee, Devin, don't go all gooey and romantic on me."

How could he have ever imagined he'd do it right? He'd missed so many opportunities with her, convincing himself she couldn't handle the realities of his life and past. She hadn't flinched, and he was still fumbling for balance. "How about I want you like crazy, and I can't go another second without touching you?"

"I can work with that." She took his hand and led him to her bedroom.

She moved some clothes from the bed to a chair in the corner, then turned, sliding her palms up his chest. "You kiss me this time."

He had last time, if she remembered, but he knew what she meant. If they were going to be together, he had to go all in. And since it was likely he'd say something else lousy, he cupped her cheek and laid his lips over hers before he could ruin everything.

She wrapped her arms around his waist and angled her head as he deepened the kiss.

He could hardly believe he finally had her all to himself, that she wanted him as much as he needed her. She was a dream he couldn't possibly hold on to, but he wasn't going to question his bounty now.

When she grabbed the hem of his T-shirt and lifted it over his head, he went to work on the buttons of her dress. In seconds, the fabric pooled at her feet, and she was left wearing a pale pink-and-white lacy bra-and-

panty set. With all that golden flesh exposed, he dug deep for restraint. He didn't usually have trouble with women and pleasure, but there was an added pressure he'd never felt before. Calla was special and pretending otherwise was futile.

He fell to his knees in front of her, kissing his way across her stomach. She slid her fingers through his hair, arching her back as he released the front clasp of her bra and his tongue wetted her nipple.

Glorying in her silken skin and vanilla-ladened scent, he wished for endless days to indulge in the need she inspired. Each sigh she exhaled and every stroke of her hands set off a fresh wave of longing. Desire unfulfilled, but assured to satisfy in short order.

When he could stand the foreplay no longer, he scooped her into his arms and laid her on the bed. She clung to him, seducing him with her mouth as if he needed more encouragement, then, smiling, she pulled a condom from the bedside table.

He snatched the protection from between her fingers and tried to take off his jeans at the same time. When he stumbled and nearly fell over, she laughed, but in a good way.

She stripped off her panties as he rolled on protection, and he found himself where he'd wanted to be from the moment he'd met her—on the verge of being part of her lightness and warmth.

"Friends?" she asked, sliding her fingertips down the center of his chest.

"Ahh…yes?"

"And more." She wrapped her hand around the back of his neck. "It's about time, Detective."

"I couldn't agree more."

As he braced himself above her, he was more sure

than ever that he didn't deserve her and completely certain he wouldn't listen to anyone who warned him off. If only for a little while she'd belong to him.

He kissed her as he joined their bodies, as the moonlight through the window illuminated their need. She both clung to him as guide and made sure he understood what she wanted.

He gave her everything he had.

She wrapped her legs around his hips and held him deep inside, bringing him pleasure like he'd never known. She wasn't a release or a conquest. She was all-encompassing, and he was in big trouble.

As they rocked and gasped for release, he knew he'd need her again. Every hour, every minute. He wouldn't get her out of his system with one night and probably not a thousand.

Maybe he'd focus better knowing she was by his side, but he'd lied going in, and she'd eventually find out. He had no intention of "getting sex out of the way." He'd stay with her every moment he could, he'd touch her every chance he got.

How could he possibly be expected to resist her light?

Her breath hitched as pleasure danced across her face. He increased his pace, absorbing her desire like a cleansing waterfall. His own climax had been hovering, but clawed to the surface as her body contracted around him. Joining her as the passion peaked, he wished for strength to keep her body satisfied, as he wouldn't hold her for long.

Wrapped around her as the echoes of their climax pulsed, she asked, "You're not going to tell me that was a mistake, are you?"

His breath still heaving, he clutched her tighter. "No way."

"Remember you said that in the morning, or you'll be back in the hospital. For an extended stay."

He smiled and kissed the top of her head. She really was remarkable.

He couldn't promise no regrets, of course. His flaws and wicked genes were bound to ruin anything beautiful they might share. But he was going to try like hell to keep her from regretting her dedication to him.

Even though he didn't deserve it.

7

In the morning, as she prepared a pot of coffee, Calla was the one wondering about mistakes she'd made with Devin.

After so many months of longing for him to admit their attraction, she still had no idea where they stood with each other. Were they a couple? Friends with benefits? Had they released that pesky tension, so now they could focus on the case against him?

They'd barely slept, and he'd shown her a tender, even playful side she'd never imagined he possessed. But the cloud of his suspension hung over everything. Now didn't feel like the time to ask him or herself—*what did last night mean?*

Taking whatever happened minute by minute seemed like the only way to handle things. Making impulsive decisions based on the heightened emotions from last night didn't seem wise. There would be plenty of time for tough questions once he had his badge back.

"Haven't we played this scene already?" he asked, causing her heart to jump as she whirled.

"I didn't hear you get up," she said lamely, soaking up the image of him, wearing only his jeans and a smile

as he braced his bare shoulder against her bedroom door frame. "Though you didn't look that happy last time."

He moved toward her. His leanly muscled body and the hungry look in his eyes caused her body to flush with heat. When he reached her, he tugged her against him and laid his mouth over hers for a long, slow kiss. "Definitely not a mistake," he mumbled against her jaw as she fought to catch her breath.

"Since when do you take my threats seriously?"

"Since you showed up at my desk, demanding I do something about fraudulent retirement schemes."

"Don't mess with Texas."

"I'll do my best." He slid his thumb across her lips. "I don't want to screw this up."

Valiantly resisting the urge to ask exactly what *this* was, Calla retrieved mugs from the cabinet and filled them with coffee. "You want eggs or oatmeal for breakfast?"

"Eggs," he answered predictably. "You really eat oatmeal?"

"It's good for you."

He sat on the counter beside the stove as she retrieved eggs from the fridge. "Too mushy."

"Naturally. Where's Sharky?"

"Passed out on the sofa."

"He got way more sleep than we did last night. Maybe we should have named him Lazy." She dumped whipped eggs into a pan. "I have some work to catch up on this morning, then I can help you. Now that we know the thief is this guy Forrester, we should be able to narrow our suspects for his accomplice and the reason he framed you."

"I'm sorry. My crappy problems are keeping you from your work."

"They're not." She glanced over to see worry in his eyes. "I need to spend a few hours in front of the computer is all. What are your plans for today?"

"I'm gonna question some of Jimmie's buddies about what he's been up to lately."

"Are you allowed to do that?"

"They won't know I've been suspended."

Calla wasn't sure about that. If Jimmie had helped set up Devin, he was keeping track of the case details. Somewhere in this mess was somebody who wanted to hurt him. Knocked out, suspended and possibly fired was a good start.

But they could hardly worry about breaking a few rules at this point.

He retrieved plates, and she served the eggs, which they ate at the bar.

"I think you should hire a lawyer," she said. She and her friends could help him investigate, but they were out of their element when it came to his legal defense.

"What for?"

"The usual reasons—to advise you, be present if you're questioned again."

"I can handle myself."

You certainly think you can. His short answers and stiff posture concerned her. Her playful lover was being taken over again by Devin the Brooder. "Okay, your call. When you're out questioning, can you swing by your place and pick up the case files? I need to know which ones involve Jimmie or any of his friends."

"Sure."

"Or we could work at your apartment if you'd rather."

He shrugged.

She pushed away her empty plate and leaned toward him. "Hey, where'd you go?"

His gaze flicked to hers. "I don't like dragging you into my mess."

"You didn't. I volunteered." The frustration over his suspension had to be draining. She couldn't imagine her career, one she'd fought for years to attain, at such grave risk. But *this*—whatever this was—wasn't going to work if he shut her out. "I want to be here." She curled her arms around his neck. "With you."

He surprised her by scooping her off her bar stool and into his lap. "I'm not used to sharing."

"You did pretty good last night." She brushed her lips across his. "Surely you're not going to tell me a cop does his best work horizontally."

"I'm a good cop."

"But not a good man?"

"I don't see how I can be."

How anyone could be as smart, strong, gorgeous and dedicated as Devin and see failure in the mirror was beyond her. "You are. Your upbringing is only the start of your life. Just because someone's parents were rotten doesn't mean they can't change the pattern. You're living proof."

His arms tightened around her. "How do you know what they were?"

"Call it a hunch." She stroked his shoulder in an effort to release the tension gathered there. "I also have a hunch you're going to need a lawyer."

"Because whoever framed me has done a damn good job of it?"

"So you have to realize this could get worse before it gets better. If everyone at the department is looking out for themselves, and they've shut you out, somebody has to look out for you."

He scowled. "I don't like lawyers."

"Sorry, sweetie, that excuse doesn't fly." She dropped to the floor, then carried the plates to the sink. "I have a..." How exactly did she describe Howard? "Well, a friend I'd like you to talk to."

Following her, Devin took the plates from her hand, then lifted her onto the counter while he cleaned up. "Who?"

Distracted by Devin's bare back—how hot was a half-naked guy doing dishes?—Calla had to stare at the ceiling before she could think again. "Howard Bleaker. He's a criminal defense attorney here in the city."

Devin dried his hands on a towel. "Shaky little dark-haired guy with glasses? I've seen him at the courthouse."

"What he lacks in confidence and appearance, he makes up for with brilliance."

"Why did you hesitate before you called him a friend?"

No way around the truth. Howard would never keep his admiration of her under wraps. She nearly regretted bringing up his name at all, but Victoria was right, they could trust Howard and he was in the price range. "I went out with him a few times. I wanted to be friends. He wanted more."

Devin crossed his arms over his chest. "You want me to hire your ex-boyfriend as my lawyer?"

"Howard was not a boyfriend."

"You dated him."

"Twice." The fierce look in Devin's eyes made her pulse flutter. "Problem?"

"Oh, yeah."

She stretched out her legs, hooking them around his waist and pulling him toward her. "Why? Jealous?"

"I don't get jealous."

"Not ever?" She flicked her tongue over his earlobe. "I think possessiveness is hot."

"Not usually," he quickly clarified.

"I could give you a minute-by-minute account of our dates."

"Please don't."

Calla's attention shifted to the floor, where Sharky sat, making noises, looking either ticked off or hungry. Probably both. "We need to get him a bell or something."

Devin picked up the cat and asked, "Eggs or oatmeal?"

"He's a guy. He wants eggs."

When she leaped off the counter and started toward the fridge, Devin snagged her hand. "Thanks for the suggestion about a lawyer. I'll think about it, okay?"

Squeezing his hand, she smiled. "Good. You'll like—"

A phone ringing stopped her comment. "It's mine," Devin said, retrieving his cell from the counter. "Antonio."

The conversation was brief, and the strain on Devin's face spoke volumes. "I'll be there" were his last words before disconnecting. He shoved his phone in the back pocket of his jeans, stroked the cat then handed Sharky to her. "I have to go."

"So I gathered. Where?"

"The station. Reid wants to talk to me again."

She set the cat on the floor in front of a plate of eggs she'd saved. "I'm coming with you."

"No. You have work to do."

"Devin—"

"They won't let you in the interrogation room." He

kissed her, an absent gesture, as his mind was clearly on the meeting with Reid. "I'll call you later."

"At least let me call Howard," she said, following him down the hall.

"No. I'm not under arrest. It's a routine questioning."

She didn't believe that for a second. Why did he? "But Devin—"

He turned, irritation plain in his eyes.

"You might want to put on a shirt first," she suggested.

DEVIN SAT IN THE HARD metal-framed chair with his hands folded on the table in front of him. He knew very well he was being watched through the two-way mirror. He was grateful they couldn't see into his thoughts.

He was in big trouble.

As if waking up in an alley with a beaten-all-to-hell thief lying beside him hadn't been enough.

They had plenty of evidence for a solid case against him. Planted evidence, but it had been accomplished thoroughly and swiftly. He'd admire the skill if it wasn't his ass on the line.

Who would go to so much trouble? And why?

The door swung open and Lieutenant Meyer entered the room. "They're going to arrest you."

"I figured," Devin said calmly, though his stomach tightened.

"Call a lawyer."

"Yeah." Thinking of scrawny Howard, he winced, but he supposed he couldn't afford to be picky. "When is Reid coming?"

"Any minute. Detective—" Meyer stopped, shaking his head as he braced his hands on the table. "*Devin,*

you know I've always supported you. You're a good cop, a valuable asset to my team."

"You know me," Devin ground out, his temper firing. "I didn't do this. I'm being set up."

"No kidding." Lines of stress appeared on Meyer's face that weren't there a few days ago. "But IAB's under pressure from the chief." He sighed in disgust. "Dirty cops are bad publicity."

Devin surged to his feet, sending the chair scooting across the concrete floor. "I'm not a dirty cop!"

"I know. But whoever set this up did a damn good job. I'm pushing Reid to continue the investigation, to continue looking into your closed cases and find a motive for the framing. He's a good cop, too."

"Sorry if I don't join you in the accolades."

"This could work to your benefit. Whoever set this up might relax when he hears about your arrest."

"It's not Jimmie."

"I agree. Maybe Jimmie will back out of testifying. You know how squirrelly he can be. Maybe he'll give up his partner. Maybe one or both will make a mistake. We need more time to get to the bottom of all this."

"Is that why Reid's doing it?"

Meyer shrugged. "Not sure. He doesn't give much away. And since he's IAB…"

"The case file is sealed to all other cops."

"Exactly." Meyer laid his hand on Devin's shoulder. "I don't need the file to work this on my own. Quietly."

Devin wasn't sure what he'd done to earn that kind of commitment and risk except close a lot of cases. If Reid found out Meyer was honing in on his case, Meyer would find himself in front of a disciplinary panel before he could blink. "Thanks," he said lamely. "I'd appreciate you passing on whatever you hear."

Meyer winked. "I imagine between the three of us, we can clear up this mess in no time."

Only three? Hell, I've got a whole gang, boss.

"Cheer up, Detective. It's not all fingerprints, mug shots and arraignments today. Your girlfriend's here."

"I don't have—" He stopped. *Calla.* Closing his eyes, he tried to use the beauty of her image to calm himself.

"She and another woman are pacing the lobby," Meyer added. "I'll send her back."

"No!" Realizing his command came out as fear, Devin clarified, "Tell her to go home. I'll call her later."

"You can actually say no to her?" Meyer asked, seeming impressed.

Devin shook his head. *Not so far.*

As Meyer left the room, Reid entered. With no fanfare and in a rigidly professional voice, he told Devin he was under arrest and recited the standard warnings.

Devin heard him as if he were underwater and Reid above. A defense mechanism, no doubt. An effort for his mind to reject what his body was absorbing.

When Reid pulled handcuffs from his pocket, Devin clenched his fists. "Is this really necessary, Lieutenant?"

"It's procedure," he said, rounding Devin so he could snap them around his wrists.

As he was led from the room, Devin wondered where Reid's backup was hiding. If he was such a flight risk, shouldn't he be surrounded? He was half tempted to struggle or even knee Reid in the gut and run. Instead, he tamped down his rage, channeling it for the moment he got his hands on the creep framing him.

Now, more than ever, he needed to lead with cold, hard facts. Not passion.

Though that plan went straight into the crapper the moment Reid led him into the hall.

SPECIAL EDITION

Life, Love and Family

Sometimes love strikes in the most unexpected circumstances...

Soon-to-be single mom Antonia Wright isn't looking for romance, especially from a cowboy. But when rancher and single father Clayton Traub rents a room at Antonia's boardinghouse, Wright's Way, she isn't prepared for the attraction that instantly sizzles between them or the pain she sees in his big brown eyes. Can Clay and Antonia trust their hearts and build the family they've always dreamed of?

Don't miss

THE MAVERICK'S READY-MADE FAMILY

by Brenda Harlen

Available this October from Harlequin® Special Edition